Richard H. Wilmer, Frederick Augustus Mitchel

Sweet Revenge

A Romance of the Civil War

Richard H. Wilmer, Frederick Augustus Mitchel

Sweet Revenge
A Romance of the Civil War

ISBN/EAN: 9783337348274

Printed in Europe, USA, Canada, Australia, Japan

Cover: Foto ©Andreas Hilbeck / pixelio.de

More available books at **www.hansebooks.com**

SWEET REVENGE

A Romance of the Civil War

BY

F. A. MITCHEL

CAPTAIN AND AIDE-DE-CAMP ON THE STAFF OF
MAJOR-GENERAL O. M. MITCHEL
AUTHOR OF "CHATTANOOGA" "CHICKAMAUGA" ETC.

NEW YORK
HARPER & BROTHERS PUBLISHERS
1897

CONTENTS

SWEET REVENGE

BUSHWHACKED

" HANDS up!"

Why he shouted the words I don't know;
for in another moment he gave me one barrel,
and before I could raise a finger I heard a
click, admonishing me that I was about to get
the other. A thin film of smoke floating
above the fence to the right and two malignant eyes peering at me from between the
rails betrayed his position. Like a flash I
whipped out my revolver, but before I could
raise it there was another report, and my
right arm dropped, benumbed by a charge of
buckshot. Seizing my weapon with my left
hand, I brought it to a level with the eyes
behind the fence and fired. There was a sound

1

of a body falling, and I knew that I had struck home.

Spurring my horse to the side of the road, I craned my neck over the fence, and there in the ditch lay the bushwhacker. His hat had fallen off, and left bare a head of red, shocky hair. In his belt was his revolver, beside him a shot-gun. His body, clad in " butternut," lay on an incline, his feet in the water, which flowed lazily past. The sun, shining through budding branches, lighted up his face, and I knew that I had seen him before; indeed, a vivid scene in which he had borne a part came up out of the past to fling over me a cloud of gloom, like the wing of an Apollyon.

I drew an involuntary sigh. It was not that I had taken a life — lives were cheap enough in those days, and he had sought to take mine; it was not my narrow escape from death; but an overpowering consciousness that the spirit of war lurked everywhere; that the beautiful face of Nature about me — trees, fences, bushes, everything — best served to cover assassins.

" Is he dead ?"

Startled at the sound of a voice, I glanced aside. There, leaning against the fence, her arms resting on the top rail, gazing at the disagreeable sight on which I had been intent, stood a young girl.

"Where did *you* come from?" I asked, lifting my hat with my left hand.

"There." She turned her head and glanced at a house on the other side of the road.

"You must have stepped lightly; I didn't hear you coming."

Without reply she continued gazing at the body of the bushwhacker. I too looked again at the upturned face, with its glassy, staring eyes.

"Why did you kill him?"

"I will tell you."

But I did not tell her then, for as I spoke I felt something warm trickling over the back of my hand, and, looking down. saw blood dripping upon her dress.

"Come into the house, *quick;* that's arterial blood."

Seizing the reins, she led my horse, I following, to a side gate. This she opened, and we went up to the veranda. Catching sight of a colored boy, she called to him:

"Mount, *quickly*, and ride for the doctor! Tell him a man has been shot, an artery cut, and a life is in danger."

I had a dim image of the boy tearing down the road, and, tottering into the house, I sat down on a sofa in the library. I must have fainted, for suddenly, without being conscious of their coming, I found myself in the midst of an excited throng. An old lady stood beside me with a basin, from which she was sprinkling my face. A white-haired old gentleman with pink cheeks, a towel in one hand, a decanter in the other, was bending over me. A boy of twelve with a toy gun was staring at me, while the girl who had brought me there looked on with far more interest than I had yet seen in her impassive face. Beyond all was a dark background of house servants. My coat had been removed, and a negro had a tight grip on a bit of wood twisted in a handkerchief tied around my arm just above the wound. A long, thin man in a rusty suit of black came hurrying in with a leather case in his hand, and, whipping out his instruments, began the work of picking up a partly severed artery. He first took out a piece of my coatsleeve, which had retarded the hemorrhage and doubtless saved my life, then a half-dozen shot, did some stitching, then carefully bandaged the wound.

"There," he said, "if you move that arm within forty-eight hours you'll be in danger of your life; keep quiet, and you'll come out all right."

"I must go on at once, doctor."

"You'll go part way as a corpse if you do."

The old lady declared that I should not stir out of the house till the doctor gave the word; the old gentleman bade me welcome as long as I needed to stay; the young lady who had brought me there said nothing; while the boy looked as if to lose a subject so fruitful of interest would break his heart.

"I'll send a young associate of mine," said the doctor. "If the wound opens you must have attention at once."

"Thank you, doctor. There seems to be a great deal of commotion about a very small matter. I don't care to put so many people to so much trouble."

No one paid any attention to my protest, all busying themselves to make me comfortable. Pillows were laid beneath my head, a silk quilt was thrown over me, a stand with a silver bell on it was placed beside me that I might ring for anything I wanted. All being satisfactorily arranged, the doctor ordered everybody out of the room, and then departed himself.

What a singular transition! Half an hour before I had left Huntsville—beautiful Huntsville, nestling among the hills that slope away from the Cumberland plateau—and was working my way northward, towards Fayetteville, Tennessee. The plants in the yards beside the road were putting forth their buds, the leaves on the trees were opening, insects were awakening, birds singing—all revived by the rays of the vernal sun.

I permitted my horse to drop into a walk. A pleasant languor stole over me, replacing a bitter mental turbulence which had been ever present with me for months. Perhaps it was the genial warmth, the balmy air; perhaps an absence of war scenes with which I had long been familiar; perhaps both. At any rate, I watched the sun glisten on the dew-drops, felt its rays warm my shoulders, and listened to the singing of the birds with a consciousness that, after all, sometimes it is pleasant to live.

Then came an unaccountable sinking. It may have been something in the restfulness, the security I had felt, incongruous with pestilent war; just as amid the luxurious foliage of the tropics one feels that behind every leaf and flower lurks invisible fever. Suddenly the shots rang out; then came my reply to the girl standing beside me looking at the dead bushwhacker; then my entry into the house; and now I was lying on a comfortable lounge, an object of tender solicitude on the part of people who, from being strangers, had suddenly become very dear friends.

But suppose they knew me—that I was a renegade, a traitor to the South. There was no name harsh enough among Confederates for those of their own people who were not with them, and all who were not with them were against them; and doubtless these new-found friends were all Confederate sympathizers. The bushwhacker could tell no tales; I was thankful for that, for he had known me well. The thought of him took me back to that night of horrors. I was again at the head of those Tennessee Unionists, endeavoring to lead them to a haven of safety. We were near the Cumberland Gap; one more day and we should be at Camp Dick Robinson, where we should find Federal troops. Then the attack. By the flashing of guns I could see their faces, and here and there recognize a neighbor—men beside whom I had lived for years, and whom civil war had converted into fiends.   One by one I saw my friends shot down.   There was one dearer to me than all besides.   Through the darkness, guided by the flashes and the sound of my voice, she darted to me, and found refuge in my arms.

Then that sudden dash of Confederate cavalry.   I felt the figure I held quiver and slip through my arms.   I moaned, and kissed the white lips.   Then like lightning the wild beast jumped within me.   I looked up to see who had done this last, this crowning atrocity.   A Confederate officer sat on his horse staring at me, in his hand a smoking pistol.   A sudden collapse, and I knew that I was hit.   This is all I remembered of the massacre.

How I gloated in my revenge!   The homes of men who had committed those murders were burning, and I had applied the torch. Their barns, grain—everything they possessed passed away in black spark-spangled clouds, which shot upward as if to carry vengeance to the very heavens.   These men had made my life a waste—I had made theirs a hell.

There was one I had not yet punished, one whose punishment I longed for more than all the rest—the Confederate officer with the smoking pistol. I sought for him without success. Then I tried to forget him; but whenever I remembered that beloved figure fleeing to me for protection, that tremor, that sinking away before the blight of death, I would start again on my long hunt. I joined the army, thinking that war's greater horrors might for a time enable me to forget my feud. All went well till I heard of *him*. He was at Huntsville. I burned to reach him. Our general was casting covetous eyes on Northern Alabama. I begged him to let me go down and bring back a report of the country—the railroads, its rolling-stock, machine-shops, bridges, everything —a knowledge of which would assist in its capture.

But this low cur who had tried to kill me. He was at the massacre. With my own hand I had applied fire to his miserable hut. How had he known that I was in Alabama? Had he heard of me during my stay at Huntsville? It had been brief, for as soon as I reached the town I learned that my enemy was not there, and, disappointed, turned my face northward. Or had the bushwhacker met me by chance? I did not know; I do not know now. Of one thing I was certain : he was one of my old enemies, and they would hunt me like a hare.

I lay for hours unwillingly turning over these war horrors as if they were a wheel on which I was obliged to tread. No one came into the room and I called no one. Doubtless they wished me to be quiet. I was weak and tired—tired in mind, tired in body, tired of existence. If I could only find *him* the world might vanish for all me.

I fell into a troubled slumber, and when I awoke I saw standing in the doorway a girl of eight or nine years—a frail, blue-eyed little thing, with her hair cut square about her neck and held by a semicircular comb. She was gazing at me intently, as children in fairy tales stand on tiptoe and look at the sleeping ogre who is intending to eat them for supper.

"Come in," I said, encouragingly.

She shrank back. But though she seemed to dread me, she could not keep away from me. Without for a moment taking her eyes off me she began to approach by slow, very slow, steps. I felt as if I were a snake charming a bird.

"Don't be afraid of me," I said ; "I won't hurt you."

"You killed *him*." She pointed like an accusing angel to the opposite side of the road, where I had left the body of my would-be assassin. Her voice was soft, but her eyes were big with the enormity of my act.

"Sweetheart, don't look at me that way; come and kiss me."

I reached out for her hand. She shrank away, but I gently pulled her to me with my well arm, drew her down, and kissed her. As I touched her pure young lips with mine the crimes of which I had been thinking—vivid as the day they were committed—seemed to move far from me, like a retreating storm muttering in the distance. And somehow, with this bit of innocence in my arm, my beard brushing her cheek, looking into her mild eyes, it seemed as if there had come a patch of blue sky; and I wished—yes, strangely enough, I wished—that it had not been necessary for me to shoot a man that morning.

II

INCOGNITO

THESE kind people with whom I was lodged persisted in considering me always in danger. A doctor must needs be at all times within reach. A stripling of a medical graduate must sleep in the same room with me. The old gentleman was constantly coming into the room to ask if I wanted anything, while his wife was as tender and motherly as if I had been her own son. Even the servants vied with each other in waiting on me, and when anything was ordered for me, with haste unusual to the negro, scrambled to see which one would bring it. Only the girl who had brought me there came and went as though I was an ordinary person with an ordinary wound, to be treated in an ordinary manner.

All this attention and sympathy vexed me beyond measure. What right had I to accept it — I, a Tennessean, in arms against the

South, in search of a Confederate enemy? Yes, and more. Was I not the bearer of information that would enable the hated Yankee to swoop down on this fair region and reclaim it for the Union? The least suspicion of my true character would turn the devotion lavished upon me to contempt. My very life would be in danger. Pooh! what cared I for my life, except that I dreaded to go to my long home detested by those who had succored me. Besides, the information I possessed—information of vital importance to the Union cause—must be carried northward.

A crisis came soon enough. It was evening, and I was reclining on my sofa looking out upon the beautiful hills lying to the eastward. The girl with the cool head and impassive face was standing by a table rearranging books and bottles and what not which had been in use during the day. Suddenly the door opened and my host entered. I saw at once by his expression that something had occurred to put him on his guard; or perhaps he had been thinking, wondering what kind of person he was harboring. At any rate, he came up, and, drawing a chair beside me, began to talk. It was plain that he wished to ask

me questions, but he was too kind, too gener-
ous to one in my condition, too hospitable, to
ask them directly.

"The doctor tells me, Mr.—" he began.
"Upon my word, you have been with us three
days, sir, and we don't know even your name."

"Branderstane, John Branderstane. I am
equally ignorant to whom I am indebted for
all this attention."

"Our name is Stanforth, sir. This is my
daughter Helen, Mr. Branderstane."

Helen inclined her head slightly, and I raised
mine far enough from the pillows to do the
same.

"Mr. Stanforth," I said — there was gratitude both in my voice and in my eyes—"whoever bears your name may hereafter call upon
me for any service. You have placed me under an obligation which—"

"Tut, tut! You know our Southern cus-
toms—we are nothing if not hospitable. You
are a Southern man, of course?"

"Of course." I spoke the words hesitat-
ingly.

"Your state?"

"Tennessee."

"East, middle, or west?"

"East."

Mr. Stanforth paused. There was no information as to my sentiments in the fact that I hailed from East Tennessee. More than two-thirds of the people of that section were with the Union.

"May I ask, sir," said my host, with an evident intention of ending all doubt in regard to the side with which I affiliated, "are you a Union or a Confederate sympathizer?"

I was about to declare myself an ardent supporter of the Confederacy when my little friend Ethel, who had visited me on the day I was shot, appeared in the doorway, her blue eyes looking straight into mine. Had my intended falsehood been rammed back into my throat with the butt of a revolver it could not have been more effectually stopped. Then something impelled me to turn my glance to Helen. She was about to pour a liquid from a phial into a glass, and had paused, her eyes fixed on me intently.

"Mr. Stanforth," I said, "you and your family have been too kind for me to deceive you. I will not do that, but it would not serve my purpose to declare myself."

"You are an honorable man, sir, whoever

and whatever you are!" exclaimed Mr. Stanforth, warmly. "It may be sometimes necessary to withhold confidence; but never to lie, sir. Keep your secret, I shall not trouble you for it. I am merely a citizen, and take no part in the national dispute."

"But I do, papa."

I looked at Helen. She was regarding me earnestly. "If this gentleman is with us," she said—"us of the South—he need not fear to declare himself. If he is with the Yankees—"

"Helen!"

There was an uncomfortable silence, during which Mr. Stanforth regarded his daughter sternly.

"If there is one right in the South," he said, "sacred above all others, it is the right of hospitality. Mr. Branderstane cannot be forced to divulge his opinions."

"But has he a right to conceal them, papa?"

"While our guest, he has."

"Mr. Stanforth," I said, "your daughter is right. No man should remain under the roof of one who has succored him without revealing his identity when it is called for. May I ask you to order my horse?"

I started up. I was too preoccupied to

notice the stand beside me covered with books, with which I had vainly tried to alleviate my confinement, and struck my arm at the very spot where I had been wounded.

A shiver passed over the father, the daughter gave an involuntary start. My coat, which had been thrown loosely over my shoulder, had become disarranged, exposing the arm, upon which every eye was turned. Both Mr. Stanforth and Helen bent forward intently. We were congratulating ourselves that no damage had been done when on the white shirt-sleeve appeared a spot of bright red blood.

" Jackson! — run! — the doctor! — *quick!* Tell him the wound has opened."

I sank back on the sofa; Mr. Stanforth began running about wildly; Mrs. Stanforth entered in wonder; the servants flocked in with open eyes and mouths.

" Papa, your handkerchief."

Helen Stanforth spoke the words as coolly as if she had been an experienced surgeon. With her father's handkerchief she improvised a tourniquet, and the bleeding stopped at once.

" Now see here," said the doctor, when he had arrived and repaired the damage, " you've

2

had a close call, sir. Perhaps you'll pay some attention hereafter to what I tell you, sir."

"Next time, doctor," I said, feebly, "let me go. My life is of little moment to me."

As I spoke, Helen, who had gone out of the room for something, returned.

"Ah, Miss Stanforth," said the doctor, "I will leave the patient in your care. You seem to be always on hand when he needs you, and to know exactly what to do. Let the others keep away."

"I will relieve you, doctor," she said, quietly.

The doctor gathered up his belongings and left the room, leaving Helen standing looking at me with a certain curious earnestness that I could not interpret. As she had been the indirect cause of my mishap I naturally expected she would refer to it, perhaps express some regret. She was thinking of an entirely different matter.

"Why is your life of little moment to you?" she asked.

"You overheard?"

"Yes."

"You have a right to require me to disclose my affiliations in the great struggle in which we are involved, but my private griefs—"

"I ask your pardon." There was no regret expressed; it was simply a well-bred way of noticing that she had failed to elicit the information she desired.

"I should have got on well enough," I continued, "if that confounded stand had not been in the way. I believe I could go now just as well as not." I paused; I was very weak. "May I ask you to hand me that glass?" I added, looking at a tumbler containing brandy.

Without noticing the proof of my inability to do as I asserted, she handed me the glass, and, when I had taken a swallow, put it back on the table. Her coolness was beginning to irritate me.

"I have a mind to get up and go on," I said. "I don't believe there is any danger."

"What did the doctor say?"

"He told me to keep quiet, as I valued my life."

"You don't value your life, therefore you will get up and go on—in other words, commit suicide."

"You know very well that it galls me to be obliged to impose upon a family that has loaded me with kindness without declaring my identity."

"Then why not declare it?"

"Because it doesn't suit my plans to do so."

I was acting ungraciously, recklessly, and I knew it; but I was in no condition to fence with this cool creature.

"Shall I leave you?" she asked, without appearing at all offended.

"I don't need your attention."

"You need some one's attention. I will have Jackson sit in the hall, where he can hear you if you ring." And she walked out of the room.

III

A DEFINITE OBJECT

"WILL this unlucky wound never heal? Time flies, and I, who should be up and doing, am caged like a tiger walking back and forth within the limits of its enclosure."

This was my complaint as I paced my room one morning shortly after the accidental reopening of my wound. My impatience was not without cause. I had gone South, as I have said, with two objects: to find my enemy and to gather information. I had failed in finding my enemy, but had gained a complete knowledge of the points essential to the capture of North Alabama, and was carrying it to the general on the day I was shot. It had occurred to me before setting out that, after finishing my military mission, I might still wish to continue my search for my enemy. Besides, there were other contingencies, such as arrest or illness, which needed to be provided for. I had, therefore, arranged that the general's favorite scout should be at Huntsville on the morning of the 1st of April to receive any communication I might find it necessary to transmit. If I were prevented from meeting him I was to send a messenger, and had devised a code of signals by which he might be recognized. The appointed day was drawing near; I was not able to keep my appointment, and there was no one at hand to whom I could intrust the message.

I chafed till I had exhausted my small store of strength, then threw myself on my couch. Little Ethel came in, and, like a soft ray of sunlight breaking through storm-clouds, turned my thoughts into gentler channels. She held in her hand a bouquet of flowers which it was easy to see she intended for me, but needed encouragement to offer. I finally induced her to do so, and to admit that she had been out a long while looking for them for me especially. I tried to unloosen her tongue, to induce her to confide in me, but in spite of all I could do she remained shy, and there was ever present that awe she had shown before of one who had taken a life.

"Why do you look at me in that way?" I asked.

She made no reply, casting down her eyes at my brown hand, which held her dimpled fingers.

"You mustn't dread me because I am obliged to fight," I continued. "These are war times; there are a great many soldiers in the land who think nothing of killing one another."

"Don't they?" She raised her eyes wide open with surprise.

"Of course war is cruel, but—but it calls out much that is noble."

"When they kill each other?"

What puzzling questions to come from such untutored lips. I was casting about for some explanatory reply when a sudden interruption relieved my embarrassment. A negro boy dashed into the room, through it, and out of another door. He was followed by the white boy I had noticed on the day of my arrival, who was screaming:

"Doggone yo', Zac, I'll break every bone in yo' consarned black body!"

The words were scarcely out when he shot through the door by which the fugitive had vanished. Little Ethel looked after him with frightened eyes, evidently dreading a catastrophe.

" Who's that ?" I asked.

" Buck."

" Your brother ?"

" Yes."

" Don't be alarmed. That's only a boy's passion ; it won't amount to anything."

" He says such dreadful words."

" That's habit ; he doesn't mean anything by it ; but it's a habit that should be broken."

I soon got her quieted, and she prattled about her dolls, her play-houses, some pet rabbits, and a nook in the garden where she kept them. How singular that war, which absorbed all about her, should have no place in her mind. Amid all the turmoil, the rumbling of cannon, the tramp of men and horses, bushwhacking, skirmishing, battles, this innocent little maid was strangely out of place. Her mother came in presently and took her away, fearing that she would annoy me. I was loath to part with her. No healing balm had been applied to my wound so soothing, so grateful, as was her prattle to my fevered brain and chilled heart.

They had scarcely left me when Buck stalked into the room, his boyish face as free from passion as if he had never been ruffled. He had made several attempts to visit me, notwithstanding that he had been forbidden the room. Seeing the coast clear, he slipped in unannounced and began a fire of questions.

"Does it hurt?"

"My arm? Yes, it hurts some."

"I'm glad yo' plunked him."

"Why do you sympathize with me instead of the other? You have only seen me a few times."

This was too much for him to explain. I could see that he had conceived an admiration for me, but he could not tell why.

"What did he try to kill you fo'?" he asked.

"Well, perhaps it was because my existence annoyed him."

"What did you want to kill him fo'?"

"I found it inconvenient to have him shooting at me."

"*I'd* like to shoot a man. I shot a rabbit once, but that's purty small game. Pop, he won't let me have a gun yet. He says I may have one when I'm sixteen."

"Buck!" called a voice from the hall. The

boy dropped behind a sofa. An old negro woman entered and looked around.

"Yo', Buck! yo' hidin' somewhar'! Yo' maw 'll spank yo' sho' ef she cotch y' hyar troublin' the gemmlen. Come out o' dar; I knows whar y' air!"

I was about to interfere; but a natural distaste at giving away a fellow-creature caused me to desist.

"I tho't I hearn dat chile talken'." The woman stood still a moment, but, hearing no sound, lumbered out of the room. The boy popped up from behind his hiding-place as soon as she had gone.

"I like *you*," were the first words he uttered. "*You* wouldn't tell on a feller, would you?"

"How could I when you are glad I 'plunked' my enemy? Is that your mammy?"

"Yes; that's Lib."

"Nursed you from a baby?"

"Yes; 'n' she reckons she's goen to nurse me all my life."

"Is your name Buckingham?"

"Buckingham! No, I 'aint' got any such doggone name as that; my name's Buckeye."

"How did you happen to get that name?"

"'Cause I was borned thar."

" Where?"

" In Buckeye."

" In Ohio?"

" Reckon 'tis the same."

I contemplated Buck for a while without hearing any of the questions he continued to fire at me. Why not intrust him with the message? There was every reason why I should *not* do so, except that he was devoted to me and I had no one else to send. While I was deliberating Lib came in, surprised him, dragged him out of the room, and shut the door.

I heard footsteps on the veranda, then in the hall, then ascending the staircase, as of people carrying a burden. The door had evidently been shut to prevent my seeing what was being done. For a while there was a hurrying to and fro, and I knew that something unusual had occurred. After all had been quieted, Buck, who had meanwhile escaped from his dusky captor, slipped back to forbidden ground.

It occurred to me that I could draw from Buck the solution of the recent commotion; but what passed under the roof of my friends was no concern of mine, and I scorned to get it from a mere boy. But I wished to test Buck's power of reticence. Ten to one he had been instructed not to talk to me about the mysterious occurrence.

"Buck," I asked, "who came to the house awhile ago?"

"Wasn't anybody came to the house awhile ago."

"A sick man, wasn't it?"

"No, he wasn't sick."

"I thought you said no one came?"

"No one did."

"Of course no one came; he was carried."

"If yo' know so much about 't, Mr. Brandystone, what's the use o' asken' me?"

"You admit that whoever he was, he wasn't sick?"

"Of course he wasn't sick. How could he be sick if he wasn't anybody?"

There was a sudden rustling in the hall, and Helen swept into the room, her eyes flashing fire.

"Buck, leave the room!" she commanded, in no uncertain tone. Buck gave a glance at his sister, which told him he had better obey, and walked out reluctantly.

"You have been listening," I said, curtly.

"I have not. I was coming through the hall and heard your last remark."

"And you infer that I was trying to get a secret which does not at all concern me?"

"I most assuredly do."

"You are mistaken. I care no more for what occurs in this house than for the color of the dress you happen to wear. I had another object in questioning your brother."

"I dare say you had."

"I wished to discover if he could keep a secret."

"I dare say you did."

"I have intended nothing dishonorable."

"Fudge!" She snapped her fingers and her eyes at the same time.

"You don't believe me. Very well; I don't believe that you were not eavesdropping."

"I was *not* eavesdropping!" she cried, hotly. "You have the word of a Southern lady."

"And I was *not* trying to get your secret. You have the word of a—" I stopped short. I had run against a snag. She gave me a glance of contempt and triumph. Her head was up, a little to one side, her nostrils dilated, her breath slow and measured.

"Miss Stanforth," I said — I was near betraying what demanded secrecy—" I will prove to you before night—no, not before night, but soon—that I had another object. I will no longer remain in a house the inmates of which—" I made a step towards the door.

" Mr. Branderstane !"

" Miss Stanforth !"

" In addition to sailing under false colors, you are now going to endanger your life by—"

" Fudge !   What is my life to you ?"   I snapped my fingers.

" A good deal just now.   It is unpleasant to have a person die on one's hands."

I was in no condition for this encounter. A buzzing was going on in my ears, a tingling sensation in my limbs.   My knees were giving way, and I was obliged to sit down on the sofa. I looked longingly at a bottle of brandy that stood on the table, but was too proud to ask for it.   In a moment Helen had poured some of the liquor into a tumbler and held it to my lips.   I drank a reviving draught; she put her hands on my shoulders and gently forced me to lie down.

" This must not occur again," she said. " You have no strength to go, and I have no

right to excite you while in your present condition. I believe what you told me." She
put out her hand.

"Pardon," I said, humbly. "When calm
I would as soon think of accusing you of
eavesdropping as I would accuse Diana of un-
chastity. I have been ungallant, rude—rude
to a woman."

"Forget it. Lie still, and you will soon be
yourself again." She sat down by a table
and took up a book. "I will sit here and
read while you recover your strength."

She read for perhaps half an hour. I supposed she was interested in the book, for she
turned one page after another and seemed to
have forgotten me. At last she put down the
volume, and by her first words convinced me
that instead of being interested in it she had
been thinking of my puzzling identity.

"I want to ask you one question."

"Ask it."

"Where did you come from the day the
shooting occurred?"

"Huntsville."

She had asked the one question and had received her reply. I knew by her expression
that she wanted to ask another.

"I suppose you were there long enough to become acquainted with the city. It's a beautiful place."

"I was there a week."

The limit of one question having been overstepped in this indirect fashion, it was easier for her to proceed.

"What were you doing there?"

"Looking for some one."

"A man?"

"Yes."

"What for?"

I did not reply at once. I was thinking of some plan by which to put an end to her catechising.

"If I tell you," I said, presently, "will you promise to ask me no more questions?"

"If you prefer that I should not."

"You wish to know why I was seeking my man at Huntsville?"

"I do."

"You will keep what I tell you a secret?"

"Yes."

"To kill him."

IV

WON OVER

LITTLE Buck had stood my test as to his reticence so well, and I was at such desperate straits for a messenger, that I resolved to use him. After breakfast I waited for a while, hoping that he would come to my room; but as he did not, and I feared he was deterred by the autocratic Lib, I called Jackson and told him to tell the boy I wished to see him. I took a Confederate bill from my pocket and handed it to the darky, but he went off grumbling "that he didn't want no Yankee money, and mas'r wouldn't hab no niggar o' his'n taken' money from a stranger nohow." He sent Buck to me, who came in looking somewhat astonished that I should take sufficient interest in him to call for him.

" Buck," I said, "I have something important to say to you."

" What is it, Mr. Brandystone?"

3

"Branderstane. Please don't make that mistake again."

"I won't, sho."

"Buck, I'm thinking of sending you on an errand; but it's a great secret."

The boy's eyes grew as big as saucers. I looked at him for a few moments to observe the effect of my announcement, and then went on.

"If you should tell any one, it might cost me my life. You wouldn't tell, would you?"

"Tell! Why, sooner 'n tell I'd—I'd—ruther be a—a—a—dead rat out in the back yard."

"I believe I'll trust you. Do you know the road to Huntsville?"

"I reckon so; I've been over it more 'n a hundred times."

"Got a pony?"

"Yes; 'Pete.' Hel'n, she drives him in the buggy. She calls him hern, but he isn't, he's mine. I got a big dog, too."

"Never mind the dog. Could you get out your pony and ride into Huntsville without any one suspecting you were going on my account?"

"Well, now, why don' y' give me somet'n hard?"

"Go and get me a newspaper or an almanac."

He was out of the room and back in a moment with a Huntsville paper of that morning's issue. I scanned its columns before looking at the date, and noticed this item:

"The main body of the Yankees are marching from Nashville to Columbia *en route*, it is supposed, to Pittsburgh Landing, where they will doubtless join the Federal General Grant."

Looking at the heading, I saw that the date was the 1st of April.

"Now, Buck," I said, "get out your pony; then come to me for instructions."

"Look a-hyar, Mr. Brandy—Brandystone—"

"Branderstane."

"Well, Mr. Brandinstane, if you got any 'structions I reckon yo' better give 'm to me now. Mebbe if I come back hyar that doggone ole Lib 'll come in 'n yank me out."

"You're right. Reach me that sheet of note-paper and a book to write on— that thin one; now a pencil. All right. Don't say a word till I have finished."

I wrote a message in as infinitesimal characters as I was able, on a third of a sheet of paper:

" Machine-shops at Huntsville in good order. Fifteen to twenty locomotives. Nearly a hundred cars. No force in the town. To the east, road runs parallel with and near the pike for several miles and is handy to cut. To the west, party to cut the road must pass round the city on the north. Enemy gathering all possible forces at Pittsburgh Landing, but several thousand men at Chattanooga."

I put neither address nor signature to it, as none were necessary, and they would be conclusive evidence against me if the message should fall into the wrong hands.

" Buck," I said, " mount your pony and ride to Huntsville. A few minutes before twelve o'clock go into the Huntsville Hotel; you know—the big brick house on the square. Go up-stairs and out on the front gallery. At twelve o'clock a man with black eyes, long hair, and a pointed beard will walk out on the gallery. Don't say anything to him; wait, and after a while he'll say something to you."

" Will he?" asked the boy, his eyes full of wonder. " What 'll he say?" .

" He'll say, ' It's a fine day.' "

" What! If it's rainen'?"

" Yes; rain or shine, if he's the man you want, he'll say, ' It's a fine day.' Then you must say, ' Reckon you're weather-wise, stranger.' To that he'll reply by asking you what kind of weather it was the day of the massacre."

"What massacre? What's a massacre?"

"Never mind that. Stick to the lesson I'm teaching you. You must say, 'Black as night.' Then he'll say, 'What's the word?' and you can hand him this note. Now, suppose I'm the man with the pointed beard and you go through the dialogue with me."

I put him through his lesson till he had learned it perfectly; then I sent him away with the injunction that in case anything should go wrong with him, rather than part with the paper he was to swallow it. I rolled it into a ball and put it into the lining of his hat. Giving his little hand a squeeze, I bade him go, and he marched out as proudly as if he had been appointed Military Governor of Alabama. I had no doubt he would execute his mission to the best of his ability, but he was very young, and I feared he would make some blunder.

"What a fool I am!" I exclaimed, as soon as he was gone. "I should have failed to communicate rather than intrust so important a matter to a boy. However, I'll leave here to-morrow morning, and if my message miscarries, by the time it's discovered I'll be somewhere 'else."

Helen came in soon after Buck's departure and began to set the room to rights. She attended to her work silently, and did not even look at me. I watched her as she moved about, arranging a curtain here, moving a chair there, or piling books on the table more neatly. She was a true type of a Southern woman—tall, willowy, a head set on her shoulders in a way to make an artist involuntarily reach for a brush. Her hair and eyes were as black as night, while on her cheeks was a bright color. There was something on her mind. I could see that plainly. I fancied if I gave her time it would come out. At last she dropped her work and stood looking out of the window.

"What are you thinking about?" I asked, going at the subject with brusque directness.

"The man you came to Alabama to kill."

"You would shield him?"

She kept her eyes on the road, watching a wagon that lumbered by. "I don't know whether I would or not."

"You want to know all about him?"

"I do."

"In the first place, you would like his name?"

"It might be well to begin with that."

"Then I can't begin, for I don't know his name."

"Not know his name?"

"No."

"What is he like?"

"Tall, well built, square shoulders which he throws back, like an officer in the regular army of the United States."

I paused. She waited for me to continue.

"You would also like to know whether his death would bereave any one: a father, mother, sister—some woman who hangs upon every word he says when he is with her, and dreams of him constantly when he is away?" I spoke the words bitterly. I was thinking of my loss.

"Yes, I would like to know that too."

"I can't satisfy you. I have seen him only once, and then at a distance."

"Does he wish to kill you?"

"No; I don't believe he is aware of my existence."

"Singular," she murmured, thoughtfully.

Then she turned and looked me in the face. "He has occasioned you some great sorrow— done you some mighty wrong?"

"You promised to ask me no more questions."

"True. I beg your pardon."

Another woman would have pouted, coaxed, done everything but asked openly to have her curiosity gratified. Helen Stanforth was made of sterner stuff. She stood looking out of the window without another word. I waited till I was satisfied that she was too proud to ask for favor, then started in again with the purpose of watching the development of some other mood.

"You are heart and soul a Confederate?"

"I am."

"And you will not excuse those Southern men and women who differ with you?"

"Yes, if they do it openly."

This was a cut at me which I did not care to notice. "Have you ever seen," I asked, "men forced at the point of the bayonet to enter the Confederate army? Have you ever seen families, trying to leave the South to join those with whom they affiliated, shot down in their tracks?"

" You are a Union man, or you would never talk that way," she interrupted.

" I was born and bred in Tennessee."

" Yes, in East Tennessee."

" May I not have seen great wrong done, and yet given my heart and soul to the Southern cause ?"

" You may, but have not."

She was getting too near the truth. I must throw her off the trail.

" I will impart one more piece of information with regard to myself. You have promised to ask no more questions and have kept your promise; you deserve a reward."

I took from my pocket a letter and held it up to her. It was addressed to

MAJOR JOHN BRANDERSTANE,
—th Tennessee Cavalry
Murfreesboro, Tenn.

Her face lighted. She did not know there were Tennessee regiments in the Union service. " I knew you were a soldier, and now I know you are a Confederate." She put out her hand, but I did not take it.

" No, no," I said, " I will not take an unfair advantage of you. That evidence is not conclusive. I have shown it to you to prove that

I may be what I will. I could offer as good proof that I am a Yankee."

"I don't care who you are, you are an honorable man."

"I see no reason for you to assume that."

"You have said it would be easy for you to prove to me that you are what I wish you to be?"

"Granted."

"But you will not. You have reason to remain unknown. You have a great purpose. You have been robbed of some one you love. You have suffered from some of those outrages in East Tennessee that papa has told us about. There has been a cowardly murder. You will be revenged. I know it; I feel it."

She was splendid in her indignation, her sympathy. I protested against this burst of confidence, but to no purpose. Were I the veriest demon in Moloch's train no one could convince her of it. I was not learned in the ways of women, but I had gained an insight into this girl's nature. Though it smouldered, it was emotional. No light kindling could set it aflame. There must be some strong underlying impulse. The purpose that I had revealed to her had taken hold of her imagination.

But it troubled her that I should withhold
my secret from her. She gave me an appeal-
ing look.

"Why do you not trust me?"

"I do trust you. Am I not at your mercy?
Should you inform the authorities that you
have an unaccounted-for man under your roof
I should be arrested at once."

"I would never do that."

"No; but will you aid me in remaining in-
cognito?"

She was silent. There was evidently a question which she was trying to solve. "Would
that be helping you to kill your man?" she
asked.

"Suppose it would?"

There was a dangerous glitter in her eye.
Perhaps she experienced a fascination in being
thus indirectly a party to my work of vengeance.

"You have not answered my question," I
said.

Still she was silent. The blood was coming
and going Aurora-like on her neck and cheek.
Presently she drew her lips together tightly
as if she were striking an enemy—

"I will."

V

ARREST

"HAVE you a man by the name of Branderstane stopping with you?"

I heard the words spoken at the front door
in a pleasant voice, in which there was something languid. My heart began a vigorous
thumping. Looking out of the window I saw
a troop of Confederate cavalry at the gate, and
men darting in different directions. I knew
that the house was being surrounded. Helen
went out to meet the inquirer.

"Do you wish to see Mr. Branderstane?"
she asked.

"I do."

Helen must have suspected that I was in
danger. There was a slight pause, in which I
fancied she was deliberating what to do.

"He is in a critical condition," she said.
"He was wounded recently. Is your business
with him important?"

"*Very* important."

"Show the gentleman in, if you please, Miss Stanforth," I called.   I knew there was nothing to be gained by attempting to put the man off.   I must appear unconcerned.

She led the way to where I was.   A young man in the uniform of a Confederate captain entered.   He was a handsome fellow, with an indolent, self-indulgent air, and evidently a gentleman.   He was extremely deferential to Helen, carrying his hat in his hand and bearing himself as if it pained him to thus trespass upon the household.

"Are yo' John Branderstane, sir?"

"At your service.   And you?"

"Captain Beaumont, —th Georgia Cavalry, sir."

"What can I do for you, captain?"

"I must trouble you to get up and come with me."

"On what authority?"

"My own, sir.   It has been reported to me that a Southern man working in the Yankee interest is here, and I have come to take him."

"Don't you think that an arbitrary way to treat a citizen of Tennessee, captain?"

"Not when he has Yankee affiliations."

"By what right do you accuse me of Yankee affiliations?"

"You were watched all the time you were at Huntsville, sir. There was no evidence against you, and you were allowed to leave the city; but after you had got away a man came forward who claimed to have seen you in one of the Yankee camps at Nashville."

"Indeed? Did he explain his own presence there?"

This was a home-thrust. The captain hesitated.

"It seems to me, captain," I added, following up my advantage, "that you are hasty in acting on such information."

Helen spoke up: "My father was at Nashville soon after the surrender. Would you arrest *him*?"

"The information comes pretty straight. I reckon you'll have to come along."

"His wound is liable to open," said Helen, "and if it should there might be a fatal result."

She spoke with apparent indifference, but she could not avoid betraying some interest. The officer looked up at her with a pair of soft brown eyes inquiringly. I saw at once that he suspected a tender relationship between us, but he was too well-bred to tread upon so delicate a matter.

"He can remain where he is until he is better," he said, bowing to Helen, "if you will give me your word—the word of a Southern lady—that he shall not leave your house till we call for him."

Helen cast an inquiring look at me to know if she should give the pledge. I saw that a glance would enable me to remain where I was, and if I chose, after the departure of the troop, leave the house, with Helen to bear the responsibility of my going.

"Nonsense, man!" I said, rising. "Do you suppose I'm going to permit a woman to stand between you and me? You are a gentleman, if you *are* taking it upon yourself to arrest whom you please. And I'm enough of a gentleman not to avail myself of your proffered avenue of escape. If I must go, I must. Where do you intend to take me, captain?"

By this time several men who had followed the officer pushed their way into the room. I received no reply to my question, but was ordered to get up and go with them. The members of the family, discovering that something had gone wrong, flocked about, and it was easy to see that though they did not understand why I was arrested, they were all in sympathy with me. Mrs. Stanforth seemed greatly distressed; Mr. Stanforth attempted to argue my case for me—of course to no purpose; the negroes were all indignant. While waiting for my horse I heard Lib delivering herself in the back hall:

" Wha' fo' dat mis'able osifer wid he sleeves covered all ober wid dem gol' snakes goen' t' 'rest a fine South'n gemmlen like dat? Dat wha' yo' call freedom? Colored folks got mo' freedom den dat. I hea'h mas'r talken' 'bout 'stutional libe'y. Wha's de use o' 'stutional libe'y when de oder man got he hand on yo' collar?"

I heard no more, for I was conducted out to the gallery. Just as I started down the walk Ethel appeared with curious eyes, and I paused to take her up and give her a parting kiss. I cast a glance at Helen. There was intense interest in her face, but among so many emotions I could not discover which predominated. I went with the soldiers down to the gate, where I found my horse, and, mounting, a cavalryman on each side of me, rode away with the troop.

We proceeded up the pike for a short dis-

tance, then, crossing the railroad track, struck
a road which bent to the east.

"Captain," I said, "I don't like the direction you are going. If your intentions were
not murderous you would take me to Huntsville and examine into the charge against me.
It appears that you are taking me into the
country to dispose of me."

"I am on my way to join my squadron near
Brownsborough, sir, where yo' will have an
opportunity to face you' accuser. If yo' are
innocent yo'll have no trouble; yo' can enlist in my company."

"Thank you; do I look like a man who
would go begging for a commission?"

"I beg yo' pardon, sir;" and he lifted his
hat apologetically.

I had retained my coolness thus far, but I
confess I did not like the situation. As a
Southern man, used to Southern people, I felt
a certain confidence; yet if it were known
that I was a Union officer I would be put out
of the way without benefit of clergy. Who
was the man who had informed against me?
What did he know? The more I thought
about it the more intense became my anxiety.
Suddenly I looked up and saw white tents.

4

I knew at once by the looks of the camp that it contained one or two companies of cavalry. There was a railroad bridge near by, crossing what I knew to be Flint River, and I judged that the cavalry was guarding this bridge.

I had forgotten my unlucky wound and was intent on the camp, when, passing under overhanging branches, a stiff bough scraped my arm, and I felt at once that it had been injured. I told the captain of my fears, and we halted to make an examination. Taking off my coat, there, as I expected, was a stain of fresh blood on my shirt-sleeve.

"You needn't trouble yourself to murder me," I remarked; "that wound is a better enemy than all my others together."

The captain cast glances about him for a house. He had no intention of murdering me or being a party indirectly to my death. While he was making a survey of the surrounding country I was twisting my handkerchief above the wound.

"Can you get to that plantation?" he asked.

I looked up and saw a large manor-house about half a mile distant, with its flanking rows of negro huts.

"I can try it."

We mounted and rode on, and in a few minutes passed into the gateway between imposing stone posts, proceeding by a winding way to the house. I was glad to dismount and get inside the spacious hall out of the sun. There I sat down on an old-fashioned, hair-cloth, mahogany sofa.

A number of white and negro children, who were playing together as contentedly as if the pickaninnies were not the property of their fair-skinned playmates, stood gaping at me. A slim man with a determined mouth, at the corners of which were marks of tobacco juice —he turned out to be an overseer—an equally thin elderly woman, whom I heard addressed as Miss Pinkley, and a quadroon girl made up the group. I was sitting with my head resting against the sofa-back, weak and despondent. Suddenly down the great winding staircase came a young girl with a shapely petite figure, a pretty oval face, and an olive complexion, from which two almond-shaped eyes flashed at me and the group about me with the quintessence of astonishment. Running her words together in a way peculiar to herself, she asked:

"What's the matter?"

"The gentleman's bleeding from a wound in the arm, Miss Jack," said the quadroon girl.

"Who is he? What is he? Is he going to die?" She fired the words as if they were bullets.

"Jaqueline," put in the elderly lady called Miss Pinkley, "don't ask so many questions at once." Then she went up-stairs, remarking that she would bring her smelling salts.

"I don't think I'm going to die just yet," I said, smiling encouragingly at the young girl, whose interest I had excited. "I received a wound a few days ago and have had very bad luck with it. Anything that hits me never fails to strike the tender spot."

"Why don't you lie down? Cynthia, go get pillows."

Cynthia, the quadroon girl, was engaged at that moment trying to drive away the children, and did not at once obey.

"Cynthia, go get pillows!" repeated Miss Jaqueline, stamping her foot.

It occurred to me that this young girl possessed an unbridled disposition. Cynthia, who was doubtless used to her mistress's way of speaking, went for the pillows, and when they arrived Miss Jack made me lie down, whether I would or not, and covered me with a shawl, sprinkling me all the while with such a warm shower of devotion that, despite her irate order to her maid, she quite won my heart.

Looking out through the hall door I saw a fat man bestride a lean horse, with saddlebags, wiping the perspiration from his face and riding up to the gallery. He dismounted and entered, puffing for breath, and proved to be a country doctor. Putting on a grave face, he examined my wound critically, and made great ado at dressing and bandaging it; then delivered the usual admonition. He departed, leaving me lying on the sofa, Miss Jack beside me, ministering to wants that were not wanted, devising schemes to meet requirements that were not required. Suddenly the two guards attracted her attention. They had been in the hall ever since my arrival, but had not until this moment excited her antagonism.

"What are you doing here?" Though her words were spoken sharply, her voice was soft and musical.

"On guard," replied one of the men.

" This isn't your house. Go 'way from here."

" Hain't got no orders."

" I give you orders." Fire was beginning to dart from her eyes.

I interfered. " They are only doing their duty."

" They have no right in this house."

" But if you drive them out they will take me with them."

" Will they?" Her manner changed. " Never mind," she said to the guard, " please don't leave us; I wouldn't have you go for the world. You're quite ornamental : one on one side of the door, the other on the other side, like statues; men-at-arms in castle halls."

The men looked at each other foolishly and grinned. The girl went up to one of them and asked him to let her examine his carbine. He did not quite like to let it go, but she took it without saying " by your leave."

" What a funny gun ! How short ! How many times can you fire it off ! I wonder if I could shoot with it !"

She brought it up to her shoulder, and, after pointing it to the wall, levelled it first at one man, then at the other. They both looked a trifle nervous, but said nothing. Then she made a motion to cock it when the muzzle was covering one of the men, and he protested. She burst into a merry laugh.

"What a brave man! Can't stand being pointed at by a girl! Ever in a battle? What's it like?"

The soldier made no reply, but reached for his carbine, and seemed very much relieved when she suffered him to take it. There was no more play, for at that moment we heard the sound of horses' hoofs, and, looking out through the hall doorway, I saw two men riding up to the house. The one was Captain Beaumont, the other Tom Jaycox, the bitterest of all my Tennessee enemies, and upon whom I had visited most summary punishment for the part he had taken in the massacre. In another minute they had dismounted and ascended the steps of the gallery, then came rapidly through the hall. Captain Beaumont's appearance denoted that there was something on his mind of great moment. His companion lumbered along beside him with the appearance of one looking for something or some one of peculiar interest to him. He was a short, thick-set man in corduroy trousers, a double-breasted vest, open, no coat, and a broad-brimmed straw hat, the hue of which indicated that it had served for several summers. His nose had been broken, and he had lost an eye. A coarse, stubby, brown-and-gray beard grew on his chin. An uglier specimen of the poor white of the South could scarcely be imagined, and the moment I saw him, knowing of his enmity for me, I gave myself up for lost.

"There he is," said Captain Beaumont.

"I reckoned so," replied the other; "he's yo' man."

"Who is he?" asked Miss Jack, quickly.

"A renegade from the South, an abolition hound—one o' our East Tennessee dogs. What he's doen' hyar I dunno, but I reckon he's on some errant fo' the Yankee gineral at Murfreesboro."

Suddenly all the careless, indolent demeanor of the captain deserted him. With true Southern impulse, without stopping to investigate the charge, he was fired by the story that he held in his hands one who, though a Southerner, was hunting information for the detested Yankees.

"Guard!" he called.

The two men approached.

"Take him away and see that he doesn't get back here. I don't want ever to see him again."

I was stunned. I knew well what this order meant. I had heard it given in case of outlaws, and knew that it was the form in which orders were given to take men out and shoot them. Many a guerilla received his sentence in those words.

"Captain," I cried, "if you shoot me you will commit a murder! That man"—pointing to the brute beside him—"is the real murderer. I know him well. I saw him shooting down women and children. I saw him—" I stopped short. There was an incredulous look on the captain's face. I knew that my accuser had his confidence. I realized that denials and counter accusations were expected from one in my position, and would have no weight.

Jaqueline, though she could not have understood the captain's order, from my words and from my stricken appearance realized the situation. She stood paralyzed, but only for a moment. While the guards were advancing towards me she stole up to the captain and slipped her arm through his. When he looked

down at her she was gazing up into his face
with the perfection of coquetry.   I watched
the effect eagerly.   His first expression was
one of surprise, then all severity died away;
an amused look followed, mingled with admiration, and at last he broke into a pleasant
smile.

VI

AN AMATEUR SOUBRETTE

I HAVE seen men disarmed in various ways: by argument, fear, force; but never have I seen one so quickly vanquished as he who was about to rush me off to execution. His intended act was most unwarranted, and had he been induced to refrain by logical arguments I should not have been surprised. But Jaqueline knew nothing of logic or the merits of the case. She used no plea; she conquered by a look.

"What a queer man!"

"Who—I?" The captain's smile broadened.

"Queerest man I ever saw. What do yo' want to take him away fo'? Don't y' know he's wounded, and we just got him fixed up?"

"You don't mean it!" He spoke as deferentially as if the information were really a surprise to him.

"Don't want ever to see him again? What

a grumpy thing you must be! Suppose I'd say I wanted never to see *you* again?"

"You'd break my heart."

All this was not to the liking of the captain's companion. "Well, captain," he put in, "what y' goen' ter do? Goen' ter let him lay thar to be coddled by the fambly?"

"Yo' hush!" cried Jaqueline, with suddenly flashing eyes. The man started back. Possibly he was unused to such quick transitions. "Yo' can't take him away till his arm gets well. 'Spose he bleeds to death? You'd have his blood on yo' hands. Just think of that!"

Considering that they had intended to take me out and shoot me, the warning was, to say the least, amusing. Every one burst into a laugh; indeed, I could hardly refrain from joining in it myself, notwithstanding my critical situation.

"You certainly don't want to commit a gross blunder, captain," I remarked. "You can at least give me some sort of a trial."

"Reckon I can refer the matter to headquarters," he replied, fixing his eyes on Jaqueline.

It was a delicate scale that balanced life and death in war time, and often required only

a feather's weight to turn it. It had been turned, for the time, and turned effectually. The
guards were ordered back, and the captain
sauntered away with my accuser, who ex-
postulated as they passed out of the house
on to the gallery. Pulling a cigar out of his
pocket, Captain Beaumont sat down in a rock-
ing-chair and began to smoke as tranquilly as
if nothing unusual had happened, listening
composedly to the ruffian who was trying to
get him to shoot me. But Beaumont was now
as difficult to move, as imperturbable, as he had
been before irate, and Jaycox at last went
away disappointed. He gave me a malignant
glance before going, which said, plainly, " I'll
fix you yet."

The captain continued sitting where he was,
his head resting on the back of the rocker,
looking dreamily up at the waving branches
of a large tree set against the blue sky. Supper was announced, and Jaqueline, taking a
rose, went out, and, fixing it in a buttonhole
of his coat, led him into the dining - room.
Before passing out of sight she turned and
gave me a meaning glance, accompanied by a
wry face at her companion. As the captain's
back was turned, it was safe for me to indulge

in a smile. Indeed, I fear I could hardly have refrained had his face been towards me. This little Jaqueline was certainly unique.

While they were at supper I was deliberating upon the situation. It was evident that my old enemies had either stumbled upon me or had learned of my presence in North Alabama, and were bent on my destruction. It was a desperate case. I was an officer in the Union army, within the enemy's lines, in citizen's dress, and in that enemy's hands. I was hounded by men who would not scruple to use any means to get me into their power. If I did not escape from the Confederates I should hang; if I did escape I should be murdered.

Presently Jaqueline and the captain came out from the supper-room, Jaqueline in advance, the captain's eyes fixed on the pretty figure before him. Jaqueline was very graceful, very dainty. Her every motion was charming. She was so light on her feet that she seemed scarcely to touch the ground. Though she walked, she danced, while her eyes danced with her body, her lips wearing a perpetual smile. Once she took two or three steps, turning half around—a mere suspicion of a dance

—a delicious, tantalizing bit, like a sip of rare wine.

"I'd like to meet yo' in a ball-room," remarked the captain, languidly.

"Why so?"

"Yo' would dance beautifully; yo'd make a charming partner."

"I can sing."

"Can you?"

"Yes, and play. One day I was playing Ginger's banjo behind the barn. Papa called, 'Yo' Ginger, stop that infernal twanging!' Wasn't it funny?"

She laughed; the captain laughed; I laughed. There was something very catching about the little minx that neither of us could resist.

She drew an arm-chair close beside the sofa on which I was lying, and insisted on the captain seating himself in it. He demurred, but Miss Jack would have it so, and the man, who half an hour before had ordered me out to be shot, was sitting by me as though we were excellent friends. Jacqueline seated herself in a rocker directly in view of both myself and the captain, and, rocking vigorously all the while, chatted like a magpie. The captain settled himself within his comfortable seat, asked permission to smoke, and, finding that he had but one cigar, insisted on my smoking it. Of course I refused, but he was too innately well-bred to smoke it himself without another for me. Miss Jack solved the problem by standing before him with a lighted match till he was forced to yield.

Then from without came the jingle of a banjo. Jaqueline caught the sound and stood listening, her head poised on one side, her eyes sparkling as though forgetful of everything save the music.

"That's 'The Bonny Blue Flag'!" she exclaimed, and she hummed the words in a sweet though by no means strong voice. As she went on she sang rather than hummed, becoming more and more animated, keeping time by patting her foot on the floor. I glanced at the captain. He was looking at her admiringly, the charm enhanced at hearing a war-song dear to every Confederate soldier, given with so much spirit by such an attractive creature.

Suddenly the music stopped.

"Don't yo' like music?" asked Jaqueline of the captain. "*I* do—I love it."

"I like it when warbled by such attractive lips," replied the officer.

Then the banjoist without played a Spanish dance. Jaqueline's body began to vibrate. But, though alive in every limb, she did not dance. There was something tantalizing in a promised treat that was not realized.

"Dance!" cried the captain, an expectant look in his handsome eyes.

"Shall I?"

"Do, please," I put in.

As a bird that has been soaring slowly sails away in its expected course, Jaqueline passed from comparative rest to motion. In another moment she was moving about the hall with improvised steps, as though dancing was, to use a paradoxical expression, her normal condition of rest. She floated, drooped, rose, rested, keeping time with her head, her arms, her whole body. For a while I was so delighted that I forgot all except the dance, and when I bethought myself to look at the captain it was easy to see that the thrall Jaqueline had been weaving about him was complete.

"Jaqueline!"

Miss Pinkley had entered the hall and stood looking at her severely. Jaqueline stopped as

5

suddenly as if she had been moved by electricity and the current had been turned off.

"I'm astonished at yo'," said the lady. "Yo've made the acquaintance of these gentlemen only this afternoon, and here yo' are dancing befo' them as if yo' were a soubrette in a theatre."

"My dear madam," I interposed, "you have no idea of the pleasure she has given us. She would be a grand success on any stage."

"Do yo' think so?" queried Jaqueline, triumphantly. "I'd love to dance on the stage."

"Jaqueline!" again cried Miss Pinkley.

"What's the harm, auntie? I'm not on the stage."

"Yes, but you want to be. To think of a Rutland on the stage! Yo' pa would be mawtified to death."

She passed up-stairs, and Jaqueline began again to rattle on in her singular way. Suddenly it struck her that she wanted Ginger's banjo, and, calling Cynthia, she sent her for it. Then, after testing the strings, she began to play and sing. The music was light but sweet, being composed chiefly of those unique negro melodies, born under the slave system as delicate plants sometimes spring up among poisonous weeds.

Without warning she put the banjo down and began to talk again, skipping from one subject to another, astonishing us by her confidences, sometimes asking questions but seldom waiting for an answer. Presently I spoke of my stay at the Stanforths.

"The Stanforths!" she cried. "Do you know 'em?"

"Yes; do you?"

"Ought to; they're my cousins. Did you see Minerva?"

"No. Who's Minerva?"

"Her real name is Helen. We called her Minerva at school. I went to school with her two years. She's older than I, though."

"I have met Miss Helen Stanforth."

"If you refer to the young lady we met to-day," the captain remarked, "she's a very beautiful and high-bred woman — much like our Georgia beauties."

"She knows everything," said Jaqueline: "theology, geology, biology, psychology. Any more of 'em?"

"That's quite enough," I admitted.

"Did you see Buck?"

"Oh yes; Buck and I became quite friendly."

"Friendly! Buck was born to be hanged."

"What makes you think that?"

"Most fiery, pestiferous little imp yo' ever saw! Doesn't stop at anything."

"Mere flashes of a strong nature. When he grows up he'll control it and be all the stronger for it."

"Think so? If he was black and I owned him, I'd have him whipped every day."

A colored woman came in and told the captain that Miss Pinkley presented her compliments, and a room was ready for him whenever he chose to occupy it. She also informed him that I could have a room.

"Captain," I said, "I have no reason to get away from you. Indeed, I wouldn't leave your guardianship just now for a plantation. The man who has accused me is in league with others who are interested in getting me out of the way. Now if you'll permit me to go to bed without a guard I'll give you my word of honor not to leave this house till after the watch has been resumed to-morrow."

"Now, captain," put in Jaqueline, before the officer could reply, "let the poo' man go to bed."

" Fo' yo' sake?" he asked, looking at her
with an expression half admiring, half comical.

" Fo' my sake, fo' yo' sake, fo' everybody's
sake."

She went up in front of him, and, putting
her little oval face within a few inches of his,
brought her snapping eyes to bear on him, and
stood waiting for his decision.

" Well, I reckon I must let yo' have yo' way.
Yo're too pretty to qua'el with."

She clapped her hands. " I knew it! Love-
liest man I ever met! Too sweet for anything!"

The captain smiled that pleasant, indolent
smile of his, looking at me at the same time, as
much as to say, " What a deliciously odd
creature," while Jaqueline disappeared as suddenly as an actress who had finished her part.
Ginger came in with a decanter and glasses,
which he placed on the table. The captain
sat down before the wine and invited me to
join him.

" Miss Rutland is ce'tainly a dainty little
thing," he said, as he took the stopper from
the decanter and filled our glasses.

" She certainly is."

" Most charming creature I ever saw."

" What a soubrette she would make !"

" Ravishing. Fill yo' glass, sir; ravishing. Do yo' know, I never saw mo' graceful dancing on the stage ?"

" Nor I."

" And what a sweet little voice !"

" The notes of a bird."

By this time I had made up my mind that it would be impossible to get the captain on any other subject than Jaqueline, and he talked of her the rest of the evening—indeed, till he had finished the decanter. I could not but be amused at the transition Jaqueline had wrought in his treatment of me. It occurred to me to test his good-nature still further.

" Captain," I remarked, " I'm caught away from home with a thin pocket-book; could you let me have a hundred dollars till I can get to where there is a bank ?"

" Certainly, sir, with pleasure; no trouble at all," and, pulling out a thick roll of Confederate bills, he tossed them over to me.

" Captain," I said, pushing back the bills, " I don't need money. I only wanted to see if it were possible for a man to order another out to be shot in the afternoon and do him a favor in the evening."

"My dear sir," he replied, "permit me to apologize for my hasty action. I give yo' the word of a Geowgia gentleman, that had not that delightful little creature interposed I should now deeply regret the execution of my order."

"You mean my execution."

"Yo' very good health, sir, and that of the little lady."

The decanter was empty. Ginger, the majordomo, appeared, assisted the captain up-stairs to one of the main chambers in the centre of the house, then conducted me through a hall to a wing, and ushered me into the apartment intended for me.

VII

MIDNIGHT

WHAT faded splendor! All the furniture was mahogany; the bed, a huge four-poster, canopied; the bureau high and with brass handles to its drawers; the chairs straight-backed; from the centre of the ceiling hung a chandelier of glass pendants. All this antique magnificence was lighted by the single tallow dip which also glistened upon the honest face of Ginger.

"I hope yo' berry comfolem, sah," said Ginger, setting down the candle and turning to depart.

"No doubt of it. Wait a bit; I want you to tell me to whom this plantation belongs."

"Cunnel Rutland, sah."

"Been in this family long?"

"A t'ousand years, sah."

"What?"

"Don't know nothen' 'bout counten'; spec

it's been in de fam'ly mighty long time. Cunnel Rutland, he mighty fine gen'l'man, sah.
Cunnel Rutland, he own ten hundred t'ousand
acres—"

"How many?"

"De biggest plantation in all Alabama, sah.
Cunnel Rutland be de biggest—"

"Wait a bit, Ginger. Who is Miss Pinkley?"

"Missy Pinkley, she mighty fine lady, sah.
Missy Pinkley, she—"

"What relation is she to Colonel Rutland?"

"Missy Pinkley, she war Missy Rutland's
sistah, sah. Missy Pinkley, she—"

"Where is Mrs. Rutland?"

"Missy Rutland, she's daid."

"Who is Miss Jaqueline?"

"Missy Jack, she's de fust young lady in de
Souf, sah. When Missy Jack go to de planters'
balls, and de city balls in Huntsville, she tak'
all de young men away from de udder young
ladies, an' mak' 'em all mad 'nuff to eat her up."

"She is Colonel Rutland's daughter, I suppose?"

"Yes, sah. Missy Jack de apple ob Cunnel
Rutland's eye, sah. Cunnel Rutland don' care
nuffen 'bout nobody but Missy Jack."

" How about you colored people?"

" What dat, sah?"

" Do you like Miss Jaqueline?"

" Like Missy Jack! Reckon de culled people do like Missy Jack. Culled people lub Missy Jack like de angel ob—"

" Isn't she just a bit hot-tempered?"

" Reckon Missy Jack *is* hot-tempered, sah. Missy Jack, she got de hottest temper in de whole Souf. Missy Jack, she—"

" Hold on; explain why you all love Miss Jack when she has a hot temper and speaks to you so sharply."

" Laws-a-massy, she don' mean nuffen. Missy Jack, she scol' wid de firebrand in de eye, but she won' let nobody else scol'. Yo' ought to see dat gal when Mars'r Bingham — Mars'r Bingham, he de oberseer — Mars'r Bingham whip de niggers. One day Mars'r Bingham he whip me. I yelled like a killed nigger. Missy Jack, she run out wid her hair a-flying and her eyes a-shinen', and she tak' de whip out o' Mars'r Bingham's han', an'—golly Moses! —how she lay it on dat oberseer!"

" Did he take it kindly?"

" *He* couldn't do nuffen; ef he tech Missy Jack, Cunnel Rutland shoot him. Cunnel Rut-

land, he got de biggest temper, 'cept Missy
Jack — ain't nobody got temper lak Missy
Jack in—"

"Any more Rutlands?"   .

"No, sah. Ain't dat 'nuff — all dem mighty
fine people?"

"Quite enough. Now you may go, Ginger."

Ginger departed with a frown that I should
have called for more such people as the Rutlands, and somewhat disappointed, I fancied,
at not being able to impress me with the magnitude of the family temper. I closed the
door behind him and locked it.

"John Branderstane," I said, looking at the
dim reflection of my body in one of the great
mirrors, "had it not been for that little girl
down-stairs your being would now be no more
real than that image.` Never have you had
so close a call, and you'll never have another
so close without it being the last. But you've
no time to waste. Your situation will be more
critical with the rising sun than it is this minute. Something must be done."

I went to a window. It was at the end of
the building. My room was on the second
story of the house, at no great height from

the ground. I turned from the window to another facing the rear; they were all open, for the weather was warm and sultry. At this second window was something which attracted my attention at once—a tree growing so near that I could easily step into its branches and descend to the ground.

"Thank Heaven, here is an avenue of escape!"

But my pledge.

It is questionable if those moral heroes who prefer death to dishonor would choose the former if the alternative were presented as it was to me. Death in the form it awaited me certainly looked very ugly. If I kept my word and remained till morning my identity was sure to come out. If fortune enabled me to conceal it, if the captain permitted me to go my way, I was sure to fall into the hands of my enemies. By leaving in the night I could give both the slip, and by morning be far away or so disguised that I should not be recognized if found. I might possibly reach the Union lines.

I had never before broken a pledge; but I had never before seen certain death staring me in the face. In the ordinary affairs of life,

I reasoned, one should have a high standard, but in a matter of life or death— Besides, who ever heard of one carrying information in war stopping at a lie or the violation of a pledge?

Placing my foot on the sill, I was reaching for a branch of the tree without when I suddenly stepped back into the room, sat down in a chair, and buried my face in my hands. A vision of Ethel Stanforth, sweet, gentle, innocent, stood before me. As a flash of lightning will clear a murky atmosphere, my human reasoning vanished before a divine intuition. I could not break my pledge.

Then I fell to thinking. How difficult it is, after all, to look into the future; who knows but some new outlet may occur to-morrow? This captain is a singular man, and no one can tell what whim may seize him next. To-day he ordered me out to be shot; to-morrow he may send me away from my enemies with an escort to protect me. Then there is little Jaqueline. She has slipped a noose about his neck that he will not easily shake off. She may find a hiding-place for me, or an avenue which will eventually lead to safe-ty. I was so pleased with the probabilities I conjured up that I got up and walked back and forth, rubbing my hands with satisfaction.

Fool! stupid human fool! The events fate had in store for me were nothing, as my foresight had painted.

I heard a tramp of horses' hoofs coming through the gateway. Going to a front window and looking out, I saw two figures on horseback. It was too dark for me to distinguish them; though one was very small, the other seemed to be a woman, for I could see her garments fluttering. They came cantering down the roadway to the gallery, and must have dismounted, for soon I heard a knocking. Leaving the chamber, I went through the hall on tiptoe and stood at the head of the great staircase, listening. There were voices below, but I could not tell whose they were. I waited some time for more information, but those who were talking went into another part of the house, and I was obliged to return to my room unsatisfied. I sat down again and renewed my musings—musings that were not of the pleasantest.

I had not sat long when two men passed under the window. They were talking in a

low tone. The voice of one was that of a
white man, the other that of a negro. The
negro said something which was inaudible;
then the white man asked:

"Which wing?"

"Dar."

Is not that Jaycox's voice? It is; there is
no mistaking that harsh growl. What can it
mean? Ah! I see it all. He expects that I
will elude this easy-going captain, and he will
spread a net for the bird before it flies. Fort-
unate! If I had descended by the tree I
should have dropped into his embrace.

My anxiety was now more intense than
ever. The cords were surely drawing about
me.

"Nonsense!" I said to myself; "I'm losing
my head. True, I'm in a tight place; but
tight places are interesting. Men who pos-
sess great presence of mind are best fitted to
escape great dangers. When the cards run
high the coolest wins. I propose to defeat
all these converging enemies by keeping my
head. I shall go to bed and get a good sleep.
Then on the morrow I shall be in shape for the
fight."

My resolution, together with the fatigue of

an eventful day, brought slumber sooner than
might have been expected. But I soon awoke,
and, having awakened, was wide awake. I sat
up in bed. I could look out of the window
into the tree which had invited me to descend
by its branches. I thought I saw a dark
object that did not belong there. The leaves
were not far enough advanced to conceal, nor
young enough to fully reveal any object hidden there. The night was not one of the
darkest, yet there was a little light—starlight,
and no moon.

"Imaginary terrors!" I muttered. "Go to
sleep."

I lay down, drew the sheet up, tucked it in
at the back of my neck, and obeyed the command I had given myself by passing back into
slumber.

I dreamed that I was standing under a great
glass receiver, and a man was working a pump
to exhaust the air. At every stroke I felt less
able to breathe, till at last I was suffocating.
I awoke, and was conscious of some one stuffing
a cloth into my mouth. I tried to cry out,
but could make no sound. Two men stood
beside me, one gagging me, while the other
began to tie my hands. This done, they

carried me, impotently writhing, to the window.

"Bring them clothes, Pete," said one of the men; "he'll give us away without 'em."

It's Tom Jaycox! I'm lost!

The man called Pete snatched my clothes and threw them out on the ground below. Then the two began the work of getting me through the window. Jaycox, who had the strength of an ox, seizing my wrists, while the man behind pushed. They got me out into the limbs of the tree, where, if I continued to struggle, I was in danger, bound hand and foot as I was, of pounding the earth below. I made a virtue of necessity and permitted them to lower me. Once on the ground they hustled me to a clump of trees back of the house, where I was unbound, and, covered by the muzzles of two revolvers, forced to put on my clothes. Then they rebound my wrists and ran me behind the barn, where two horses stood ready saddled. Jaycox took me in his steel arms and tossed me on to one of them with as much ease as if I had been a bag of meal. The two men mounted the other horses and we started off, circling around back of the negro huts and under trees to a side gate

6

opening on the pike.   Once away from the
grounds we set off at a gallop.

Kidnapped!   Now I *may* save myself any
further worry.   The inevitable is before me.
Before daylight I shall be a dead man.

VIII

ON THE PLATEAU

On, on we sped, under starlight, over stony pike, steel-shod hoofs striking fire on flinty stones, snake fences writhing, trees dancing in a semicircle about those beyond. We dashed over wooden bridges; we splashed through shallow streams; we dipped into hollows and tilted over crests, while now and again some startled bird stretched its wings and went whirring into the forest.

On my right rode Tom Jaycox, holding my bridle-rein, his ugly face turned always towards me. Every crime-moulded feature—his cold, steel eye, his knitted, overhanging brows, spoke one word: "Vengeance!" On the other side galloped a man, long, lean, hungry, grinding uneasily on a quid. I did not know his name, but memory brought me a picture of that same face lighted by shot-guns flashing in the night.

Our breakneck speed lasted till we had put some miles between us and the plantation, then we slackened our pace and walked our panting horses till they had partly recovered their wind, then struck a trot. It was immaterial to me at what gait we moved, I thought only of my approaching end. Surely it could not be far distant. Why did it not come at once? A pistol-ball, a club—anything is enough to take a life. Then I shuddered as the thought struck me that I was to be kept for a more lingering death.

We were passing between a range of hills on our left and the Cumberland plateau on our right when Jaycox drew rein and we all came to a halt. There was a sound of horses' hoofs behind, coming at a brisk canter; but no sooner had we stopped than the sounds ceased. Both the men listened until all was silent, then Jaycox started on.

"All right, Pete," he said. "Whoever it is has either stopped or left the road."

"Some un goen' home late, I reckon."

We proceeded on our way, but had gone scarcely a quarter of a mile when we again heard the hoof-beats in our rear. Again we pulled up and listened.

"By gosh, Tom," said Pete, "thet beats me!"

"Shet up!"

Both listened, waiting to hear the sounds renewed, but as they were not we started on. For the second time the hoof-beats recommenced, and this time a little nearer.

"We must git outen this," said Jaycox. "Let's take to the hills here instead o' furder on."

Turning to the right we passed through timber, beginning a gradual ascent of the plateau. Jaycox rode ahead, holding my bridle-rein, while Pete followed, revolver in hand.

Who were on the road I knew no more than my abductors, but as a drowning man will catch at a straw I cast about for some method of letting them know of our digression. Bending low in the saddle, I peered through the gloom, watching for something with which to produce sound, for my gag prevented my shouting, and a shout would have brought punishment. Coming upon a flat rock, by a pressure of the knees I guided my horse over it, but it was too firmly imbedded to be moved. Soon after I encountered another, right on the edge of the trail. Digging my heels into my horse's flanks and throwing my body out of equilibrium I forced him to prance. A vigorous pull on my bridle-rein by Jaycox saved him from going over the incline, carrying me with him. But I had accomplished my purpose. I heard the stone go crashing down the mountain.

"You infernal dog," cried the man in the rear, "ef yer do thet agin I'll run a knife atwixt yer shoulders!"

"Ef he does 't agin yer needn't trouble yerself to stick him; the fall ud finish him."

Higher, higher, we mounted, farther from the dark plain below, upon which here and there shone a lonely light; nearer to the patches of fleece in the heavens, and the stars looking down from above. Then came a faint light in the sky and a gray tinge over the country below. Woods, streams, fields, houses, barns, grew out of the darkness. The light broadened, there were gilded clouds in the east, the sun cast its first beams over the heights and upon the landscape below. We had reached the upper level; we were on the plateau.

Espying a log-house ahead, the men consult- ed, and determined to try for some breakfast. They took the gag out of my mouth, and as soon as I was free to speak, anxious to be at once put beyond suffering and the terrible suspense of an impending murder, I cried:

"You dogs! you cowards! you're going to kill me! Why do you delay?"

They looked at each other knowingly and grinned—a horrible, soulless grin.

"D' y' reckon yer goen' to git ter heaven without payen' fo' th' damage y' done?" snarled Jaycox, with an ugly light in his eye.

"Ah, that's your game!"

"We know you uns ter be as well fixed fo' property as any young man in Tennessee. An' we're goen' to hev a slice too. But yer needn't reckon thet's goen' ter save y'. Yer got ter shell out, 'n then—" His look told the rest.

"Give me one shot with my back against a tree, and I'll fight two such cowards as you."

"Shet up!" snapped Jaycox, showing his teeth within a foot of my face, and with a glance like that of an angry bulldog. Then, riding up to the entrance of the hut, he shouted:

"Hello thar!"

An old woman came to the door with an iron spoon in her hand.

"Wall, what's wanted?"

"Snack."

"Hain't got nothen' but pone."

"Got any coffee?"

"Coffee? D' y' reckon Abe Lincoln's goen' ter let us hev coffee away up in these mountings, when they hain't got none down in th' towns? I got a yarb 'll do purty wal, though."

My captors dismounted, breakfasted, then arranged for a short nap, one watching while the other slept. Jaycox first sprawled himself on the ground, and was asleep in a twinkling, while his comrade sat staring at me with his gun ready cocked. I knew that if I made the slightest movement with a view to escape he would shoot me. Occasionally he looked impatiently at a handsome gold watch—doubtless taken in spoil—as if anxious for the expiration of his hour of duty. Towards the last he nodded. I was near some low bushes and began to roll towards them. He awoke with a start, and, quick as a flash, brought his gun to his shoulder.

"Yo' hound!"

Jaycox opened his eyes, and, seeing a murderous look in his companion's face, and a gun right over his foot pointed at me, kicked the weapon upward, discharging it, thus doubt-less for the time saving my life.

This finished the first watch, and Jaycox took his turn, admonishing me that if I tried the experiment again he would tie me up by the thumbs. I dreaded this torture, and gave him no cause to enforce it; besides, he kept awake during his entire watch.

The men having secured the needed rest, we broke our bivouac, Jaycox loosened the horses, and his companion kept me covered with his gun while I mounted. As I put my foot in the stirrup I happened to glance aside and saw two horsemen approaching. In a moment I recognized Buck Stanforth and Ginger. How they came to be there was a mystery. I only knew they were there, and rejoiced. At seeing me Buck was about to give a shout, when he bethought himself that such a proceeding might be fatal, and regained his composure just as his presence was discovered. Ginger showed no signs of recognition whatever. I shot a quick glance at Jaycox, to see if he recognized the negro. To my relief he did not appear to know either Buck or Ginger.

"Say, yo' men," called Buck, "can we get somepin to eat hyar?"

"Ef thar's any vittels left," said Jaycox. "What you uns doen' out this time o' day?"

"Oh," said Buck—I trembled lest his wits should desert him at a critical moment—"I'm taken' this nigger to his new master. He's sold."

"Yer a peart 'un ter d'liver a nigger; reckon he don't mind goen' with yer."

Buck and Ginger dismounted as we departed. I was obliged to part with them without being able to utter a word or make a sign. Still their presence gave me hope. Hope! What could a simple negro and a boy do to rescue me from two stalwart brutes who were watching me like cats?

All day we moved northward, the men riding close beside me, now and again turning their ugly faces towards me with a grin of satisfaction, or a scowl when I did or said anything to displease them, often bending close to me, sickening me with their rank tobacco-smelling breaths or the worse odor of their unwashed bodies. We met no one. The only comfort I derived was from the natural objects of the mountains. A red fox stole away under cover, a chipmunk, fearless and free, sat on a log, looking at us curiously as we passed. A budding wild rose brushed my boot; it was like the kiss of a loving companion. Even the twittering birds seemed to be offering sympathy.

Towards evening, as the sun stood just above the horizon, a dull red ball, a shadow resting on the lower landscape, one of my captors gave a whoop. It was answered by a man ahead, and in a moment a dozen more started from about a camp-fire.

"Got him?" yelled the foremost of the group.

"Yo' bet!"

With a cheer every man sprang for his gun.

"Hold on thar!" roared Jaycox, with his bull's voice. "Don't yer be fo'gettin' we're goen' ter be paid fo' our losses fust."

A man by no means as repulsive as the rest, slenderly built, with a weak mouth, long, black hair, and a beard through which shone a tinge of color on his cheek, stepped to the front as with authority, and it was soon evident that he was in command. He inquired about certain of the gang who were lurking about Huntsville. Jaycox mentioned the name "Ike," though I could not hear what he said, whereupon the captain turned and glanced at me. I inferred that Ike was the man who had tried to kill me, and whom I had killed for his pains. Then the captain and Jaycox went into a thicket near by, evidently for consultation, and were followed by the others, while I remained behind, still sitting on my horse, and watched by Pete, who stood on the ground, a great gaunt figure, one hand holding the bridle-rein of his horse as he nipped the grass, the other grasping a cocked revolver. He was looking at me from under his faded sombrero, his eyes peering into mine malignantly, his jaws grinding on his quid, the juice of which soiled the corners of his mouth. I could not endure to look at him, and turned towards the landscape below. The sun had set; it was the beginning of night. Was it not the beginning for me of the eternal night?

IX

FIENDS

It was plain to me that I was in the hands of that terrible war-time scourge of the South, the guerrilla. This band had been made up in East Tennessee, and had moved out of their original stamping-ground to get away from their old homes, and find a better field for pillage. From the Cumberland plateau they could swoop down towards Nashville, Murfreesborough, McMinnville, Shelbyville, Fayette, or Huntsville, and, if chased, could easily take to the mountains, where it was difficult to follow them. On one of their forays Tom Jaycox and Pete Halliday had got wind of my whereabouts, and, with several of the gang, including the man I had shot, had gone down to look after me. The country in and about Huntsville was too civilized for open assassination, and Jaycox, after the failure of the attempt on my life, had procured my arrest as a spy. Then followed the plan to kidnap me and force me into a payment of money before the final revenge.

We bivouacked where we had met the band on the plateau, under the trees that waved above us, their sprouting leaves lighted up by our camp-fire. I lay awake the greater part of the night, watching for an opportunity to escape, but one sentry after another was placed over me, and morning came without my having made the attempt.

At sunrise we moved northward as on the day before, my captors still keeping a strict watch over me. During the day Jaycox pushed on in advance; why, I did not know, but surmised that his going had something to do with the plan to plunder me.

The mountains seemed deserted. Not a human being did we see save two women and a negro, all on horseback, travelling in the same direction as ourselves. I caught several glimpses of them, though always at a distance, and wondered how it was that "poor white trash," to which class they appeared to belong, could afford the attendance of a slave.

When we halted for the night, which we

did about five o'clock in the afternoon, the captain came up to me and told me they were going to take me to a point near my old home, Knoxville, where I would be required to sign a check for a large amount—all they could squeeze out of me; but if there were not sufficient funds to my credit in the bank, I must execute papers that would enable him to con- vert property into money. If I would do as he wished he would set me free. This I knew to be a lie; the gang would find a pretext to murder me whether I signed the document or not.

He left me sitting on the ground, leaning against a log, contemplating the horrors of my situation. If I did not pay my ransom I should be murdered; if I paid it I should be murdered; it was Hobson's choice. I made up my mind that I would attempt to escape, get shot, and thus end a situation that was in- flicting on me a mental torture far greater than any physical pain mortal ever endured.

Casting my eyes inadvertently towards the road, I saw two women passing northward, and in another moment recognized them as those I had noticed on the march. To my sur- prise, one of them turned and rode towards us;

the other hesitated, started on, turned, and followed her companion. I noticed something familiar about their figures. The coarse text-ure of their jackets and gowns, and their unbecoming sunbonnets were out of keeping with their graceful carriage. "If these women knew," I thought, "that they were entering a guerrilla camp they would be stricken with terror." When they reached a point a dozen yards distant they paused, the one in advance calling, in a harsh voice:

"Can you uns tell us how fa' 'tis t' Tracy?"

Then, beneath the homely check bonnet, through the olive darkening of her complexion, under the cheap calico, I recognized Helen Stanforth. Her quadroon companion was none other than my fascinating little friend who had saved me from the impetuous wrath of Captain Beaumont—Jaqueline Rutland.

Had a pair of angels come down from heaven and lit on my shoulders I could not have been more astonished. I rubbed my eyes, thinking that my vision deceived me; but when I looked again there was Helen sitting on her horse, chatting with the guerrillas as if they were ordinary persons, making common-

place remarks in excellent dialect, with which
a long residence near the mountains had made
her familiar. Jaqueline remained a short
distance behind her. For a while I feared
that Jaqueline would betray them both,
for I could see that she was trembling. But
presently all terror seemed to leave her. She
rode up beside Helen and began to chaff the
men, at once attracting the attention of the
whole band.

"Yo're a likely gal," said one of them. "Git
down offen that critter and stay awhile."

"Couldn't think on 't."

"Oh yes, y' kin." And he walked up and
took hold of her bridle-rein.

"Yo' Jim Canfield," cried the captain, "let
that gyrl alone !"

The captain advanced and invited the two
visitors to alight, promising that they should
be respected. Jaqueline gave him a grateful
look as he helped her off her horse with far
more gallantry than might have been expected
from the leader of this gang of ruffians. Indeed, there was something in his bearing to
make me suspect that this bandit captain—
Ringold they called him, though I suspect the
name was assumed—was an unworthy mem-

7

ber of some good Southern family who had
disgraced himself with his peers and become a
leader of those who were, like himself, devoid
of principle, but in other ways his inferiors.
Jaqueline must have divined as much, for no
sooner was she on terra firma than she slipped
her arm through his and clung to him confid-
ingly.   Pete Halliday, who seemed to be the
next member of the band in importance after
the captain, awkwardly attempted to gain
some mark of her favor, but Jaqueline, with
woman's quick intuition, knew that if any one
was to be relied on it was Ringold, and declined attention from any other.

"Who ar' yo'?   Whar did yo' come from?
What yo' doen' hyar?" she asked, in her usual
quick way.   "Hain't yo' goen' t' join our boys
'n' fight fo' th' 'Bonny Blue Flag'?"

The captain looked a bit uncomfortable, and,
as she had asked several questions to which a
reply would be in order, he replied to none.

"Can't yo' sing the 'Bonny Blue Flag' fo'
'em, Jack?" asked Helen.   "Reckon yo'd like
ter hear her," she added to the group; "she's
right smart at singen'."

"Reckon," said Jack.   "D' y' want ter
hear 't?"

The men were too stupid, or, rather, had not the politeness, to say they did. They stood and gaped. Jack, who I could easily see, under her enforced gayety, was badly frightened, made a desperate effort and began to sing, but her voice was so thin and trembling that I thought every moment she would break down. However, when she came to the last stanza she had regained something of confidence, and ended the song pretty well.

She had scarcely finished when we heard a picking of banjo strings. I looked up and saw a boy and a negro advancing towards us. I was not long in recognizing Buck and Ginger, the latter thrumming the instrument as he came on.

"Whar's a house fo' t' git supper?" called the boy.

"Dunno; hunt yer own supper," replied one of the men.

"Hain't you uns got nothen' thar t' spar'?"

"Reckon; but we hain't goen' ter spar' 't."

Buck started towards the camp, and Ginger followed him.

"I'm a-taken' this nigger t' Sparty; he's sold."

"Hain't y' got that nigger offen yo' hands yit?" called Pete Halliday.

Buck looked at the speaker in assumed surprise. " Wal, now, you uns mus' be th' men we met yistid'y   Hain't yo' got yo' man offen *yo'* hands yit ?"

A grin passed over the faces of the men.

" Don't yer mind 'bout that man," replied Pete Halliday, " er yer'll git inter trouble."

" Whar does the nigger b'long?" asked the captain.

" I'm taken' him ter Sparty."

" Y' don't keep him under close watch," said Pete.

" Oh, he hain't no runaway nigger. He's got me in charge 's much 's I got him. He's b'longed to the fambly since befo' I was borned."

By this time the travellers had reached the camp, Buck's intelligent face contrasting with the stupid look which the negro was assuming.

The man who cooked for the band was busying himself preparing supper. With one accord the two girls took hold to help him. He at once dropped his implements and gave way, while all stood gaping at the unusual sight of two women who, unmasked, were cooking a meal for them. Helen occupied herself over the fire and managed an iron skillet—the only cooking utensil in camp—as dexterously as a chef. Jack took the tin dishes that composed the kit and "set the table," an act hitherto unknown at guerrilla meals. Then, when supper was ready, they insisted upon waiting on the men. No one objected to this save the captain, who, by his protest, a second time indicated that he had seen better days and knew something of deference to women.

The meal ended, the girls insisted on washing the dishes. When there was no more work to do, Jack sang out:

"Clar th' way, you uns, 'n I'll give yo' a dance!"

X

A DANCE FOR A LIFE

The proposition was received with shouts of approval.

" Yo' don't mean yo' kin dance ?"

" Reckon."

" Good gal! Clar th' way fo' a dance !"

" Yo' nigger, tune that banjo! 'T's lucky fo' yo' y' got 't, strings 'n' all, er we'd 'a' made strings outen yer hide."

The camp was on a circular piece of hard ground so cut off from the sun by surrounding trees and bushes that no grass grew. The few scattered sprouts were soon cleared away; Ginger sat down on the log which lay near by, twanged his banjo, tightening or loosening a string, and then gave a preliminary flourish.

Jaqueline took off her sunbonnet, threw it a few feet away, and stepped on to the clearing. There was mingled fear and defiance in her face that set my heart to fluttering.

Though I did not know she was carrying out a preconcerted plan, somehow it got into my head that she was about to dance for my liberty —in other words, for my life. The thought maddened me. An impulse seized me to throw off the mask and defy the whole band. Helen, seeing the desperate resolve expressed in my face, gave me a look, partly imploring, partly commanding, that recalled me to a sense of my helplessness.

Jaqueline began sailing about, keeping time to Ginger's music, moving hither and thither with uncertain steps, as a bird will flit back and forth before darting away in its flight, or as a musician will sweep his fingers over a harp before beginning his melody. Gradually the music grew quicker, and Jack, gathering confidence, forgot everything but the dance.

Since the entry of the two girls into the camp I had suffered one terror after another in quick succession, and now it struck me that in case Jack succeeded in fascinating this lawless group, some of them, fired with a desire of possession, would break through all restraint. I had been wonder-struck that two defence-less girls should dare to come among them,

and now I was stupefied that Jack should
dance before them and that Helen should permit her to do so. But who shall measure the
strength of woman's weakness? Mother Nature had taught Jack and Helen their power,
and they went about their work with not a
tithe of the fright that possessed me.

Meanwhile Jaqueline had drifted into the
dance, and was whirling, bending, floating, every muscle alive with its especial motion. At
times she would lull, poise herself for a moment, then, like a fitful wind, start again with
renewed fervor. At no time could there be
discovered aught but delicate refinement in
her movements, and now it was her purpose to attract without exciting her specta-
tors. Stimulated by frequent bursts of applause and by the rapt attention of the men
surrounding her, she found her main in-
centive in a far deeper, nobler motive—feeling,
as she did, the critical situation, the dread responsibility for a human life resting upon
her.

What a singular scene? The ring of ugly
faces momentarily softened by the sight of
grace and beauty; the captain, his sharp
face turning with the dancer and following

her wherever she goes; Pete Halliday, standing with folded arms, lowering from under the broad brim of his sombrero, grinding his quid; Ginger's black face gleaming with pride at furnishing the music for his young mistress, inspiring her with his own inspired melody; little Buck, standing between two lank guerrillas in "butternut," staring at his cousin, and forgetful of her danger in his interest in her work; Helen Stanforth, standing apart, her strong face wearing the expression of a general who watches a cavalry charge intended to turn a position on which hangs the fate of the day.

The guerrillas, not one of whom would hesitate to slit a throat at the slightest prospect of gain, were watching the little soubrette, not only with admiration but with respect. Once during her performance one of the men applauded with a ribald remark. He was standing by the captain, who stretched his arm, brought it down with a backward stroke, and sent the man sprawling. Jaqueline saw the act and the approving looks of the outlaws, who were in no mood to have their sport interrupted. The color left her cheeks, but she kept right on, and the episode passed without further consequences.

At a moment when the attention of the men had become riveted upon the dancer, Helen, who had been gradually working her way from the group towards me, came and sat down on the log behind Ginger, where she was partially screened by him. Watching her opportunity, she deftly took a revolver from her pocket and concealed it in the folds of her dress. With her eyes fixed upon the group about Jack, she waited for a burst of applause, and when it came, reaching back she dropped the weapon behind the log at my feet; then, rising, rejoined the circle. I pushed the revolver under the log with the toe of my boot, then kicked dust and leaves over it. This accomplished, I breathed the most comfortable sigh of relief I have ever drawn in my life. The whole situation seemed changed by that little dust-covered combination of bits of metal. Stooping, I slipped it into the leg of my boot, and felt that half the battle was won.

At that moment the setting sun came out from behind a cloud and shot lances of light through the trees, covering the group — the beautiful and the ugly, the good and the bad, the refined and the vulgar—with gilded splen-

dor. I saw but Jaqueline. The usual fitful-
ness of her disposition, her natural expression
of careless indifference, had given place to a se-
rious intensity denoting a great purpose. Pois-
ing herself between two movements, the gilding rays shone on her forehead. Then darting on her toes to another part of the ring, a
quick succession of lights and shades passed
over her brow — a glittering diadem of sun-
flashes. Truly God is a wonderful artist, since
He can touch even a dance with celestial pu-
rity.

Helen Stanforth turned to me. Pulling her
sunbonnet forward so as to conceal her face
from the others—though they were too intent
on Jaqueline to notice her — she moved her
lips, and though no sound came I knew she
intended the word:

"Go!"

Near me was a tree; not far from that
another; underbrush, bushes—just the cover
through which to make a retreat. I could
easily get down behind the log, crawl into the
thicket, and away. Now for the first time the
purpose of dear little Jaqueline was fully apparent.

But how could I leave these friends who had

risked so much, accomplished so much, for me? I stood still and shook my head.

Again Helen looked an order for me to go.

" Not without the others," I whispered.

Sitting down on the log so as to be nearer to me, she replied, in a low voice:

" We will leave here when you are safely away. She will dance on to keep them from knowing you have gone. We have planned it so."

" They will know you connived at my escape and murder you."

" Why should they? Go at once, or I shall consider you an ingrate."

She looked so anxious, they had all made such a noble effort in my behalf, that I could not find it in my heart to disappoint them.

I slipped behind the tree, dropped to the ground, and wriggled like a snake through the underbrush; then, rising, darted away.

A dozen yards — fifty — a hundred. The music of Ginger's banjo dies as suddenly as the clang of a bell on a passing engine. Will one minute or five pass before I am missed? A distant burst of applause—God bless the dear little dancer! Before me is an open space, then a dense clump of trees. If I can reach that thicket I can make a quick digression, and this may throw my pursuers off my track.

A confusion of yells—a bullet whistling by my ear. I reach the wood and push on through it, not daring to lose distance by digression with an enemy close behind me. My feet becoming entangled in a vine, I stumble and fall. A weight comes down on me, crushing the breath out of me. It is all over.

Panting, bleeding, white as a ghost, I am led back to the guerrilla camp.

" Shoot him !"

" Gimme a rope offen that pack-mule!"

" Tie him on a critter 'n' send him down the mounting !"

A babel of brutal suggestions came from the different members of the band, sounding to me, stunned as I was, like final random shots at the slaughter of a " forlorn hope." Amid the clamor I saw but one sight—Helen and Jack locked in each other's arms, paralyzed with terror.

" Stand back, men !" cried the captain, pushing his way towards me. " Have y' forgot the money ?"

" Stand back !" roared Halliday. " He belongs to me 'n' Tom Jaycox. We tuk him."

The captain's authority, thus supported, saved me from immediate death. The men who were crowding around me gave way, a cord was brought, and my wrists and ankles were securely bound. No one seemed to suspect that Jack's dance had anything to do with my flight, except that I had taken advantage of the relaxed vigilance to make the attempt. Having tied me, they threw me to the ground, Halliday giving me a parting kick; a man was deputed to watch me, and the band, accustomed to such episodes, left me, to turn again to what was far more interesting to them.

XI

STEALING THE GUNS

JAQUELINE once more became an object of undivided interest. The men crowded about her, staring at her, uttering exclamations of admiration, vainly seeking a way to do her honor. Presently they cut saplings, out of which they constructed a rude chair, decorating it with twigs, and one ill-favored bandit, to whom nature had imparted a spark of art, gathered wild flowers with which to put on finishing touches. When the seat was completed, the men looked awkwardly at Jack, and the captain, presenting the tips of his fingers, led her to her improvised throne. Helen, who at the first sign that I was to be temporarily spared had recovered her equanimity and had infused some of her restored courage into Jack, saw at once the advantage of keeping up her cousin's popularity. Seizing some of the flowers, she wove them on a framework of green twigs into a circular garland, and insisted on crowning the favorite—not Queen of May, for May had not yet come, but queen of a month far more appropriate—April.

By this time night had come on, a roaring fire was lighted, and the guerrillas, forming a ring of which Jack was the gem, threw themselves on the ground and listened to her chat, her songs, her stories, their firelighted faces standing out of the gloom in grim contrast with her refined beauty. The captain, with his superior breeding, served as a link between her and his men, keeping them in check and stimulating their admiration by his own. If Jack flagged for a moment between her stories and her songs Helen was quick to suggest new ones, and occasionally both were relieved by little Buck, who would throw in some quaint remark typical of that peculiar creature—the American boy.

So long as the songs and stories lasted there was nothing to precipitate trouble, but the entertainment could not go on all night, and I began to dread the moment when the girls should attempt to take their departure. Presently Helen, in a firm voice, said:

"Come, it's time for us to go."

Shouts of "No!" "A dance!" "A song!" greeted the proposition, and the guerrillas began to form in groups to resist an exit. Helen, selecting the noisiest knot of men, drew a revolver from her pocket, and, cocking it, moved towards them with her eyes fixed upon them, calm and steady. Whether it was that they were cowed by the weapon, or admired this evidence of woman's pluck, they opened a way. The captain, seizing the opportunity, quickly took Jack by the hand and led her after her cousin. Once beyond the ring, he assisted the girls to mount, then, mounting himself, the three rode away, followed by a cheer. As for me, I breathed one long sigh of relief.

"Well, Ginger," said Buck, "reckon ef we uns 're goen' to git to Sparty to-morrer we'll have to travel all night."

"Is th' nigger taken' you to Sparty or air you taken' the nigger?" asked one of the men.

"Dat ain't gwine to mak' no differ," said Ginger. "Mars' Buck 'n' I don' never hab no trouble. Mars' Buck, he's my mars' till I gits to de new one."

Buck led his horse to the log and mounted,

H

giving me a significant look, as much as to say, " I won't desert you," then rode away, followed by Ginger, with the remark:

" Good-bye, yo' fellers; much 'bliged fo' the good time."

The restraint of the girls' presence being no longer felt, the men's behavior changed in a twinkling. The captain's absence left Pete Halliday—the worst man in the gang—free to foment trouble, and he began to do so by sneering at his chief for being brought, as he expressed it, under petticoat government. There appeared to be two factions in the band —the one headed by Halliday or Jaycox, the other by Captain Ringold. Halliday set about instigating the guerrillas, or, rather, his adherents, to go after Helen and Jack, and bring them back for another dance. To make matters worse, one of the men found some apple-jack, and it was not long before the gang were half drunk. Meanwhile the captain returned, and received a hearty cursing from Halliday and his adherents. Several of them started to bring back the girls, but Ringold drew upon them and threatened to shoot them unless they returned. They staggered back, grumbling, and the captain adroitly proposed another pull at the apple-jack. This diverted them, and, after finishing the liquor, one after another sank into a drunken slumber.

It was midnight. Every member of the band was asleep, save the man who was deputed to guard me. He was sitting on a piece of fire-wood, so placed that he could watch me across the flame. I lay on my back looking up at the stars and feather-like clouds that now and again floated across the great blue dome,—the only motion apparent, save the tree-tops bending under an occasional breeze. The fire flickered, the guard nodded, an owl in the distance gave an occasional hoot.

I heard something stir in the underbrush. Glancing aside, I saw a small light disk over a bush. It was the face of little Buck.

Now, in the name of all the gods, will those devoted friends never give over risking their lives in these useless attempts? What is to happen now? I scowled an order to the boy to go away, but he paid no attention to it. Something came sliding along the ground and lodged against me. The guard heard it, started, cast a quick glance at me, then about him, but, seeing nothing, relapsed into his former quietude.   I felt for what had struck me, and clasped a jack-knife.

Meanwhile Buck disappeared. but, soon appearing again in his place, held up a carbine. He had doubtless stolen it from one of the men who slept on the edge of the circle about the fire.   Again he disappeared, and I watched eagerly for his return.   The guard was still awake, though nodding, but had he been more watchful he would not likely have discovered Buck, for the underbrush, both where the boy appeared to me and where it skirted the sleeping guerrillas, was so thick that in passing around the camp he was comparatively safe from observation.   Besides, for most of the distance Buck traversed in his gun foray the guard's back was towards him.

I watch the point where Buck's head appeared, expecting to see it again, but in its stead presently see two white points.   Straining my eyes, I discern the whites of two eyes, then a black face.

It is Ginger.

A white line appears directly below the eyes, and I know Ginger is showing his teeth in a smile.   He raises his arm, and, behold! another gun.   Again a white line of teeth, and he puts the weapon down. Five, ten, fifteen minutes elapse. Ginger holds his ground. Has he gone to sleep? No. Another five minutes, and he holds up another gun. Ah, I see; little Buck, with cat-like tread, is gathering in the arms. That's well; he is far better fitted for such delicate work than a stiff old negro.

This little pantomime begins to take shape in my mind, and brings anticipations of more than a fight for my own life. If I can escape, and Buck and Ginger secure sufficient arms, it may be possible for all our party to get together and make a defence. I must tell Ginger to get some ammunition. But with a guard looking straight at me it is no easy task to convey an order by signs, and that to a stupid negro. Catching sight of a small stone beside me, I put out my hand, yawning to conceal my intention, let it fall on the stone, and soon have it between the knuckle of my thumb and the point of my forefinger, as a boy holds a marble. Watching till the guard's head is turned, looking meaningly at Ginger, I fire the stone a short distance, hoping he will understand the word "ammunition." His face is a blank; it is evident

that he does not know what I mean, and there
is no prospect of his getting it through his
thick skull.

Ginger turned away, and I knew that he
was speaking to his young master; then
Buck's white face showed itself inquiringly
behind the negro's black one. I looked meaningly at Buck, and repeated the motion of firing. He caught my meaning, and, taking up a
gun, made a motion as if ramming a cartridge,
looking at me inquiringly. I indicated that he
was right. He went away, and after a long
absence came back and held up four cartridge-
boxes, two in each hand. Then, putting down
the boxes, he held up three fingers, and I knew
that they had secured three guns. He next
held up four fingers of the other hand, pointing to the sleeping guerrillas, and I knew he
proposed to get one more gun.

Buck was a long while capturing the fourth
gun. One of the men awoke, yawned, sat up,
and looked into the fire; yawned again, lay
down, and was soon snoring. Then the guard
got up from where he was sitting. There was
a slight sound in the bushes, and he listened
attentively. Then he put some wood on the
fire and sat down again. He had scarcely

seated himself before Ginger held up the fourth gun.

I moved slightly, showing my friends by my manner that I was about to try to get away. They appeared to understand and gathered up the guns, Buck taking one and Ginger three, doing all so silently that no sound reached even me. I waited, watching the guard intently till he should nod. I had no expectation of his going to sleep; I only hoped to free myself from my thongs before he would discover my movement. He nodded; I moved; he opened his eyes; I snored; he nodded again; I grasped the knife. Thoughtful Buck! he had opened the blade. Drawing up my knees I cut the ropes that bound my ankles, then felt in my boot-leg for the revolver. I was about to cock it when I remembered that the guard would hear the click. I thought I would conceal the sound by a sneeze, but a sneeze might disturb some of the band. The owl, which had for some time been silent, hooted. It usually gave three hoots in succession. I counted—one, two, and at the third cocked my revolver. Through my half-closed lids I cast a glance at the guard. His eyes were shut. I looked significantly at

Buck and Ginger to show them that I was ready, then motioned them to go. Waiting long enough for them to put a few hundred yards between them and the camp, and noticing that the guard's eyes were still shut, I prepared to follow.

Rising slowly and silently, keeping my eyes fixed on the man by the fire, raising my revolver, and taking as good an aim as possible with bound wrists, I stood on my feet. One step backward; then another; a third, a fourth, a fifth, a sixth. I had reached the bushes where Buck and Ginger had been concealed, and was about to take one more step which would secure concealment when the guard opened his eyes and looked straight at me.

Surprise was his last emotion, my figure the last sight he ever saw. I shot him through the head, and before the report had ceased to reverberate was in the bushes.

XII

A DAYLIGHT ATTACK

Despite the thickness of the surrounding underbrush, I made quick progress. Jumping clean over bushes, darting around trees and under low limbs, after running some two hundred yards from the guerrilla camp I came to a comparatively open space. Seeing a figure standing within it, and surmising it to be one of my friends, I was about to call, when a woman's voice cried "Halt!" I knew that I was covered by a weapon, and stopped short.

"Are you—"

"Yes; and you?"

"Helen. This way."

She darted away like a deer. I soon overtook her, and together we ran perhaps half a mile, when she began to climb an ascent leading to the base of an overhanging cliff. I saw through the gloom a large and a small figure climbing just ahead of us, and knew they were

Ginger and Buck. Helen led the way up to a recess in the cliff, and I saw at once a position that we could hold against a dozen men so long as we had food and ammunition.

"Hello!" It was Jack's cheery voice. "Goody! Ain't I glad to get out o' the wilderness!"

"*I'm* glad enough," I said, as soon as I could get breath to speak; "but you women—"

There was no time for words. We set about rolling a big stone into a gap between two others, and as soon as it was in position had a continuous breastwork. The guerrillas were calling to each other in the woods below, but they did not seem to know where we were. I picked up one of the guns Ginger had thrown down, Buck had one in his hands, Ginger kept one, and Helen seized the remaining one.

"Where do *I* come in?" chirped Jack.

"Here." I handed her the revolver, in which there were five loaded chambers, and told her to hold on to it, as she would doubtless need it. We all took position behind our breastworks ready to repel an assault, at the same time seeing to the condition of our pieces. They were cavalry carbines, all loaded and capped ready for use.

"Where are your horses?" I asked.

"Picketed down there," Helen replied, pointing westward, "in a thicket not far from the road."

"Have you anything to eat?"

She glanced at a parcel on the ground. "I got that in a cabin. There's some corn-pone and pork."

"Barely enough for one meal. Any water?"

"There's some water trickling between the rocks back there."

"That pone and pork means a chance, but it's a slim one."

Helen set her lips; Jack turned pale; Ginger showed no emotion whatever; while Buck remarked that he'd be "darned if he didn't plunk one of 'em, anyway." As for myself, I was aghast at the terrible fate that threatened those who had so nobly and so bravely risked all in my behalf.

"What brought you here?" I asked, impatiently, of Helen.

"When you were taken from our house I resolved to follow. Buck came in just as I started, and insisted on joining me. We traced you to Colonel Rutland's plantation—"

"I see; it was you I heard coming in after I went up-stairs."

"Ginger took the horses to the stable, and was returning to the house when he saw two men climb a tree near your window and enter your room. He watched from a distance and saw them bring you out, but he could not tell whether they were taking you away by force or assisting you to escape. Coming into the house, he told us what had happened.

"Jack started to awaken Captain Beaumont, but I stopped her. If you had been assisted to escape this would be fatal; besides, from what Jack had told me of the captain, I judged he would have his night's rest before starting in pursuit. I told Jack I would follow you myself, and she was wild to come with me. Ginger had seen you leave the plantation, and knew the direction you had taken. We sent him and Buck ahead, and they soon came near enough to you to hear your horses' hoof-beats; then waited for us to come up. Soon after we lost track of you, but hearing something come crashing down the mountain—"

"A stone."

"We followed the direction of the sound. In the early morning Buck and Ginger came upon you unexpectedly. As soon as you had gone they rejoined us, we shadowed you, and yesterday afternoon laid a plan for your escape."

"A wild, impracticable scheme. One circumstance has led to another, each involving you more deeply. My God, what a load of obligation! We can't stay here; we'll starve. Buck, couldn't you slip out in the darkness and find help?"

"No, siree; I'm not goen' out o' hyar. I'm goen' t' stay 'n' fight with the rest."

"But you may save all our lives."

"Why don't *you* go, Mr. Brandystone?"

"I? I must stay with your sister and cousin. Besides, I'm big, and couldn't get through as easily as you."

"Well, I ain't a-goen' to sneak away if I *am* little."

"Bucky," said Jack, "yo' needn't go; I'll go myself."

"You don' do nuffin like dat, Missy Jack," cried Ginger; "dem grillers shoot y'! Wha' mars' say ef I go back an' tell 'em de apple ob he eye go down 'mong grillers fo' to git shot. *I* gwine, mars'," he added to me.

But by this time there was more calling

among the men below, a streak of light appeared in the east, and I did not dare let any one attempt to evade the enemy; besides, I could now see by the lay of the land that it would be impossible.

Something must have given the guerrillas an inkling of our whereabouts, for as soon as it was light we could see them standing, looking up at our position. I told every one to lie low, hoping that some of the outlaws would climb up to investigate, and we might pick them off. For more than an hour we remained concealed, only speaking in whispers; then we saw the knot of men below divide, three going to the west, three to the east, while three began to climb towards our fortress. One remained below, and as the light increased I saw it was the captain.

We four who were armed with carbines knelt behind the rocks, I to the extreme left, Helen next, then Buck behind the stone we had moved to fill the gap, with Ginger bringing up the right end of the line. I was an excellent shot—I had long been considered one of the best in Tennessee—and it turned out that Helen was not bad. Ginger was no shot at all. I selected the man in advance for my

especial object, designated the second for Hel-
en, and gave Buck the third. They were to
fire after me in the order named. Ginger was
to fire at any who might be left standing.
Jack had only a revolver, and I directed her to
keep back. She was trembling, and in order
to strengthen her by concentrating her mind
on some duty, I told her to be ready to hand
us the ammunition after the first volley.

The guerrillas came on, every man holding
a carbine. When they had covered a third of
the distance I saw that Buck was about to
fire out of turn, and I was obliged to speak to
him somewhat sharply. I think the advancing men heard me, for they stopped and consulted. The captain, standing below, called to
them to go on, and, separating so as to leave a
dozen yards between each man, skirmish-fash-
ion, they started again, watching eagerly for a
sight of something to fire at. As they were
all abreast, my order for firing would not
serve. I gave another.

"*I'll* take the left man, Miss Stanforth the
centre, Buck the right."

There was no response. All were too intent
on the work before us to speak. I permitted
the men to come within a hundred yards,

when, taking deliberate aim with a rest, I
shot my man through the heart. In another
moment Helen's rifle cracked, and the centre
man dropped. Buck, who was excited, fired
wild, and missed altogether. Ginger lost his
head completely, and did not fire at all. As
Ginger's courage deserted him, Jack's came
to her all of a sudden.

" Why don't y' shoot, Ginger ?" she cried,
with flashing eyes. Snatching his gun and
aiming it at the remaining man, who was rapidly getting down the declivity, she sent him
the rest of the way with a limp. Two men
were put out of the fight and the third disabled.

" By golly !" cried Buck, " we licked 'em,
didn't we ?"

I thought it best not to discourage him by
telling him that this was only a preliminary
skirmish, but asked Jack for the ammunition,
and we all reloaded.

The wounded man went back to the captain, who appeared greatly agitated over the
result. He was evidently surprised at the
reception of his searching-party. The men
who had gone to the flanks, hearing the firing,
rejoined their leader, and two men who had
been in the rear came forward.

Heaven preserve us! The captain has started up the slope at the head of a storming-party of eight men.

I was appalled. We had but four guns, and after firing a volley must reload before firing another. We could not expect to disable more than four men at the first fire, then the remaining four would be upon us before we could reload. In quick tones I gave the order:

"All load; I'll fire."

With that I let drive, and dropped a man. Then, throwing down my gun, I took Helen's, and dropped another. Buck handed me his, and I dropped a third.

"By jiminy!" cried Buck, exposing his head to see better, "ain't yo' a bully shot!" Ping! went a bullet within an inch of his ear, and he ducked.

"Keep down!" I cried, as the lead rattled against the rocks in front of us, and fired the fourth gun, again hitting my man, though I only "winged" him; indeed, I believe he dropped to evade the fire. By this time the first gun had been reloaded, and I took aim at the captain. I was sure I hit him, but he came on. Taking the next gun now ready

9

I fired at him again, but just as I did so one of the men stepped in front of him and received the shot. This finished the assault. The men broke and fled, and before I could get another shot were far back towards the position from which they had started.

BELEAGUERED

STRANGE that men will never learn the terrible advantage of a force posted on an impregnable position, protected by breastworks, and able to pour shot down a steep hill at an enemy. Two men, two girls, and a boy had defeated the guerrillas and sent them back to their camp. I did not fear another attack. What I dreaded was starvation; indeed, I could see plainly that our enemies were preparing to carry out the starvation plan. Several of them went in different directions, doubtless for food. One of them passed quite within range.

"I'm goen' t' plunk that one," said Buck.

I caught his arm and gave him a reproof which for a while, at least, caused him to remember that I was in command.

"I wish they'd attack us again," said the irrepressible boy. "I could 'a' hit that dog-

gone ' butternut ' if somep'n hadn't joggled my
arm."

There had been nothing to joggle the boy's
arm, but I thought it best to let him keep up
his pride; it would make him more serviceable;
so I said nothing.

"I aimed right at the middle of his breast,"
continued Buck, "but just then he jumped
over a stone and I missed him."

"I thought some one joggled your arm?"

"Some one did.   Ginger, yo' consarned old
nigger, what d' yo' go joggle me fo', just as I
was goen' to plunk him?"

"*I* didn't joggle yo', Mars' Buck."

"Was it you, Hel'n?"

"No."

"Somebody did, or I'd 'a' hit him, sho!"

If ever a party needed breakfast it was ours.
Helen unrolled the little parcel of provisions.
I directed her to serve a half ration, or, rather,
half of what there was, and save the rest.
She did so, handing me my portion, which I
declined, but she argued that it was important
for all that I should keep up my strength,
and finally prevailed on me to eat my share.
Jaqueline and Buck ate theirs ravenously.
Each of us went to where the water was drip-

ping from the cleft and caught the drops in
our mouths. Buck, when he had finished his
breakfast, like Oliver Twist, asked for more.
It made my heart ache to refuse him, but
there was no alternative.

One danger was dwarfed by the greater
perils that surrounded us, yet it was no less
important. My wound was liable to put me
hors de combat at any moment. Fortunately,
until my dash from the guerrilla camp, I had
not been subject to any physical strain, and by
that time it had healed sufficiently to prevent its opening—at any rate, it gave me no
trouble. The first thing Helen asked, after a
lull in the fighting, was about this wound.
She insisted on dressing it for me, and I permitted her to do so. She wound around it a
fresh bandage torn from my shirt-sleeve and
was pinning it when, looking up at me, she
said :

"You're not the first one of our men I've
assisted with bandages."

Her remark cut me like a knife. It was
plain that she was making this effort, incur-
ring this danger, believing me to be a Confederate.

"I can't understand all these troubles that

surround you," she went on. "Why not explain?"

"You know I'm charged with being in league with the Yankees."

"Yes; but your accusers are robbers and murderers. If I thought *that*—" She broke off with a frown, and turned away.

The guerrillas built a fire, and, after cooking and eating breakfast, loitered about, some chatting, some playing cards, while others devoted themselves to their wounded companions, making them as comfortable as possible on beds of boughs covered with blankets. I took advantage of their inaction to learn how Buck had succeeded in delivering his message to the scout he was to meet at Huntsville. As I could not question him before the others without giving up my secret, I drew him into the cleft behind us.

"Buck, did you find the man I sent you to meet at Huntsville?"

"Reckon I did."

"Tell me about it."

"All right. As soon as I got into town I went right to the squar', 'n' stopped in front o' the hotel. I hitched my pony to a post, 'n' went inside. A man in the office said, 'Sonny, what

d' y' want?' 'n' I said, 'I'm goen' up on the gallery,' 'n' he said, 'What fo'?' 'n' I said, 'Fo' t'
see the town.' Then I went up-stairs 'n' waited till I heard the clock striken', 'n' counted
thi'teen."

"Not thirteen, Buck. Clocks don't strike
thirteen."

"Well, don't y' see, that clock at Huntsville
's a different kind. It struck either thi'teen
or fo'teen, I couldn't tell which."

"Never mind the clock. You're inventing
all this. Go on."

"Well, just as the clock struck, a man he
came out on to the gallery. He had the dog-
gonest eyes I ever saw—just like the wolf's in
Red Riding-hood. At first he didn't take any
notice o' me, looken' 's if he was bothered
'cause I was thar, 'n' he expected somebody.
Then he watched me with those sharp eyes o'
his'n, 'n' at last he said, kind o' gruff, ''T's a
fine day, boy,' 'n' I said, said I—what was it I
was to say?"

"'Reckon you're weather-wise, stranger.'"

"Oh yes, I know; but I couldn't remember
'zactly, 'n' I said, said I, 'Reckon yo're weather-
beaten, stranger.' He stood a looken' at me
kind o' quar, 'n' I heard him a grunten'

somep'n like, 'Guess I am beat, somehow or 'nuther.' Then he asked me somep'n 'bout whether it was a raimen' at the time of the—what was that one?"

"'The massacre.'"

"Oh yes, I know. And I said—what was it I said?"

"'Black as night.'"

"That's it; only I fo'got, 'n' said, 'Black as a doggone nigger,' and he said, 'What's the—'"

"'Word.'"

"'What's the word?' 'n' I took the spitball out o' my mouth 'n' handed it to him. He took it 'n' read it mighty quick. Then he looked at me and said, 'I'll be goldarned if that ain't the littlest messenger to carry such a big message I ever saw in my life! Like attacken' a fortyfication with a how'tzer.'"

"What did he do then?"

"I don' want t' tell that."

"Why not?"

"Well, he must 'a' thought I was a baby."

"Come, out with it."

"He took me up and give me a kiss, rubben' my face with that hairy beard o' his'n."

"Then what?"

"He went down-stairs in a hurry, and I didn't see him any mo'."

"Good for you! Have you kept it all a secret?"

"Haven't said a word to any one."

"That's right. You've done me a great favor, and one good turn deserves another. I'm going to tell you how to cure yourself of that bad habit of using useless adjectives. If you ever get out of this, get a note-book and pencil, and every time you use one of them note it down. This will show you how often you offend, and at last you will break yourself of a very bad habit."

"I'll do that, by golly!"

At noon we were again tantalized at seeing the guerrillas eating their dinner.

"I wonder what they got?" said Buck. "I reckon 't's nothen' but fat pork, anyway. Who wants to eat fat pork?"

"I wish I could get my clutches on the captain," said Jack, "I'd make him give me some."

"De Lord 'll feed His chil'n," remarked Ginger. "Didn' He send de ravens to Elijah?"

"Not in these mountains." put in Buck. "Ravens couldn't find anything up here to feed anybody with."

"Reckon dat mus' 'a' been in a land flowen' wid milk 'n' honey," supplemented Ginger.

"Yo' ole fool," retorted Buck, "how could a raven carry milk?"

"Don't be so smart, Buck," said Jack. "A raven could take the handle of a tin bucket in its mouth and fly with it, couldn't he?"

Then Jack and Buck fell to vying with each other which could invent the most remarkable fabrications about the wherewithal to satisfy their hunger.

"I see a darky coming," said Jack, "with a white apron and cap, and a tray on his head covered with good things to eat."

"That's nothen'," said Buck. "I see a roasted goose waddlen' up the hill with the stuffin' tumblen' out of a hole in his breast."

"Yo' little fibber, yo' don't see any such thing. I'll tell yo' what *I* see. I see a big table down there among the guerrillas covered with smoking beef and chicken and lamb with mint sauce running all over it, and peas and asparagus. Come, let's go and get some."

She was so earnest about it that I feared she would; indeed, she started, but Helen caught and drew her back. Throwing herself into Helen's arms, she covered her face with her hands.

XIV

A BONFIRE DEFENCE

MORNING, noon, afternoon passed with no change in the situation. All my command slept during the day, and even I got two or three hours of tired nature's sweet restorer, though I would not close my eyes till Helen had promised not to take hers off the guerrillas till I awoke. During the afternoon all began to suffer from hunger, but I would not allow the scanty bit of food remaining to be eaten. Buck got over the noon meal bravely, but when supper-time came he clamored for something to eat.

"Now, see hyar, Mr. Brandystone," he argued, "you just give me my shar' 'n' I won't want any mo' when the rest of yo' have yo's."

"You must wait, Buck; we shall have to fast long enough, anyway. The longer between meals the longer we can hold out."

" All right," he said, bravely, " I can hold out as long as any of yo'."

As evening came on a horrible thought loomed up suddenly. If the night should be dark, there was nothing to prevent the guerrillas stealing up on us unawares, and capturing our stronghold.

" I *must* find a way out of this," I muttered, and began an examination of the face of the rock in our rear. The cleft where water dripped slanted upward, a narrow opening little wider than a man's body. I crawled into the crevice, and, by using hands and feet, mounted to the summit. I stood enchanted by the splendid view. Northward and eastward the Cumberland Mountains reared their heads, a succession of wooded crests; westward the fair plain of Middle Tennessee; southward, Confederate territory cut off from us by war, and setting aflame the imagination as to what was taking place in the new-born nation. An undulating horizon divided the black earth from the scarlet sky left by the setting sun.

Scrambling over the uneven ground, climbing rocks, fighting my way through thickets, I explored every promise of outlet. There was not a possible descent. I returned to the mouth of the crevice, intending to rejoin my companions. I heard some one clambering up, and, looking down, saw Helen Stanforth. Giving her my hand, I helped her to level ground.

"You and I," I said, "should not be absent from the front at the same time."

"Tell me," she said, fixing her eyes on me intently, "what I want to know. I have led Jaqueline, Buck, and Ginger into this trap in an attempt to save you. The least I can expect is your confidence. Who are you?"

Our lives depended on absolute devotion to each other. If I should tell her that I was a Southern man holding a commission in the Yankee army, that I had sent information North to enable a Union general to capture the region about her home, I should sap our main element of strength. On the other hand, I was accepting all this devotion under false pretences. The thought was maddening. Had she not been looking at me with her big, honest eyes, I believe I should have shed tears of anguish.

"Miss Stanforth—Helen," I said, " who and what I am can be of no moment now with death staring us in the face. You and I have a mutual purpose—to save those who have been led into this peril. There is no time for explanations. I beg of you to banish for the time this secret, and think only of the work before us."

She turned her eyes out to the far-distant horizon, but did not see it, intent on her own thoughts. Then, looking again at me, she said, with a burst of impulse:

"To know that you are unworthy would kill me."

I bowed my head to escape her gaze. When I looked again she had turned and was entering the crevice.

Having failed to find an outlet in our rear, we had no choice but to face our enemies. I cast my eyes over the only route open to a night surprise. On our right, not far below, was the bare face of a rock twenty feet high, around which was no path. To the left another rock projected in such fashion that while an enemy climbed over it his silhouette would appear against the sky. Noticing an abundance of fire-wood scattered about, I resolved to build a bonfire, with a view to lighting up our enemies should they attempt to steal upon us in the night. As soon as it was dark enough I sent Buck and Ginger out to gather

wood, and, selecting a flat rock midway between those on the flanks, scooped together
some light dry stuff for kindling, and as fast
as the wood was brought me put it on. When
all was ready we returned to our fortress.

But how light a fire? There was not a
match in the party; indeed, the only means of
ignition we possessed was a percussion-cap. I
sacrificed two cartridges, and poured the powder they contained into a bit of paper, intending to explode it with percussion-powder.

Night attacks always occur just before dawn,
and I felt confident that we should hear from
the guerrillas, if at all, between two and three
o'clock in the morning. At one I awoke the
command and issued our remaining ration. It
was eaten ravenously, and when the last morsel had been consumed I told all to be ready
at the slightest sound. I was going down to
the unlighted fire, and in case they heard me
hammering the percussion-powder they would
know I had heard the enemy approaching.
Then, taking Jack's revolver, I sallied forth.

I passed down to my fire-wood, inspected it
to see that it was all right, then went on farther, crawling on my stomach and listening.
Noticing what in the darkness I supposed to

be a log, I resolved to crawl up behind it for concealment. On reaching it I raised my head and looked down into the face of a dead man. It was the body of one of the guerrillas we had shot during the day. This uncanny object, encountered at dead of night, startled me. There was the ghastly skin, the sunken cheek, the open mouth, while the eyes were staring up at the heavens as if they saw wonders hidden from the living. I drew back. A consciousness of the horrors that awaited us struck me like a gust of cold wind. Perhaps before morning Helen Stanforth, or Jaqueline, or little Buck, or all of us, would be lying stiff and stark like that dead guerrilla.

Then a greater strength, a daring, a cunning never before felt welled within me. I crawled on till I came so near the guerrilla camp that I could have thrown a stone into it. They had no fire, and this in itself was suspicious. I thought I heard a voice, but it was doubtless some animal or a bird giving a note of warning to its mate. I listened, but could hear nothing which I knew to be human. At last I sat down on a rock, and began what to me seemed an endless vigil.

It was, perhaps, an hour after that I heard

unmistakable sounds of the guerrillas. I could see nothing, though I could hear voices, and voices at that time of night meant mischief. Darting back to my wood I set the paper of gunpowder on the rock under the dry grass, keeping a little in reserve, and got a stone ready to use for a hammer, then listened for a sign of advance. I had not long to wait. A man must have stumbled; at any rate, I heard something which convinced me the enemy was coming, and, laying on my percussion-powder, I raised the stone and brought it down.

Horror of horrors! The grass was blown away without being kindled. The last chance was gone! It was dark as pitch; not even a ray of moonlight to protect us against the coming cutthroats.

Wait a bit. There are several spears of grass smouldering, a spark on the end of each. I gather them, and put the ember ends into the hollow of my hand, where I hold the reserve gunpowder. A flash — a mere bit of flame no bigger than a pea! I nurse it and put more grass with it, shove it all under the wood, and a beautiful bright flame shoots up that gladdens my heart. A joyful shout from

10

the fort sends a pleasant thrill through every fibre in my body.

Ping! A bullet within an inch of my nose. I dart away into the darkness, and in another minute am in the fortress.

I had scarcely got behind the breastworks when the glare of the burning wood showed me half a dozen men dashing up to the fire, and I knew they would try to scatter it.

"When I count three, fire into the crowd. One! two! three!"

Four bullets flew at the little knot of men below. We could not see who was hit, but all turned and started down the declivity, though one man dropped before he had gone a dozen yards. We lost no time in reloading, and had a new charge ready in every piece before seeing any signs of their return. But Buck, who took more time and made more fuss about his work than all the rest together, had scarcely rammed his charge home and fixed the percussion-cap on the nipple when three men made a dash at the fire. Two of them reached it and began to kick vigorously. I took deliberate aim at one of them and shot him through the head. My gun had scarcely cracked when Helen let drive at the remaining man. He staggered, but kept on kicking at the fire. I snatched Buck's gun and finished him, dropping him on the burning brands. The third man, who had started forward several times and each time turned back, got out of sight as quickly as possible.

"Look a' dar!" cried Ginger, pointing to the east.

I turned my head, and there above the horizon was the faintest trace of dawn.

XV

WOMAN'S PLUCK

AFTER this second defeat we could see the guerrillas gathered in a knot, evidently discussing the situation. They talked so loud that we could often catch a word, and their gesticulations were plain to us all. At last the captain took a white handkerchief from his pocket, fixed it to a stick, and, holding it over his head, advanced towards us.

"A flag of truce!" we all exclaimed together.

"He's going to offer us something to eat!" cried Jack. "I knew he wouldn't let us starve."

I stepped over the breastworks to go and meet the bearer of the flag. Buck called out:

"Tell him I'll take some fried chicken fo' mine."

I met the captain at the spot where we had built our fire. His arm was in a sling and he was very pale. Something told me that he did not relish the work in which he was engaged.

"I've come to tell you," he said, "that if yo'll surrender, the rest of yo' people can go."

"What assurance have I that you will keep the terms?"

"The word of a—" He stopped. I saw that habit had led him to use an expression common among gentlemen in the South, but the word had stuck in his throat.

"Captain," I said, "you are a better man than the company you keep. Satisfy me that the women, the boy, and the negro shall go free, and you are welcome to *me*."

"The men are divided about the women," he replied, lowering his voice.

"Which party holds the balance of power?"

"It's hard to tell."

"Then we have no assurance that if we surrender you can keep your promise to let them go unharmed?"

"There's no telling. Befo' your escape and the killing yo' all have been doing I could have fixed it. But the men are exasperated at the damage you've done."

"Can't you be blind, and let us out to-night?"

"No; I've lost more control of my men within the last few days than all the time I've commanded them. If they saw the slightest move on my part to let yo' slip, they'd shoot me, and yo' would never get out alive, either. I can't stand here talking any longer. They'll suspect something. What's yo' answer?"

I turned the matter quickly over in my mind.

"Captain," I said, "I will transmit your proposition. If your terms are accepted, I will go down to your camp and my friends will follow. If they are not accepted, we will wave to you. In this event you will know that these noble girls, this brave boy, this faithful negro, prefer to take their chances with me."

Both of us turned without another word, and in a few minutes the captain was with his men, and I had joined my little half-starved army. I was received with eager, questioning looks.

"He has made a proposition," I said. "I will give it to you with the information that goes with it. If we will surrender, he promises that all shall go free except me."

I paused a moment to watch the expression

of their faces. I saw at once that they were all bitterly disappointed.

"I feel bound to state further that the captain has informed me that he cannot surely guarantee your safety, though he would if he could. He tells me that the men are divided, and he does not know himself which party is the stronger. You are not sure of safety, but you have a chance, whereas if we are taken by force the chances are all against you. Before giving my own views, I wish to get an expression of opinion from each one of you separately. Miss Stanforth, shall we accept the proposition or not? Say yes or no."

She curled her lip. "I don't care to consider such a proposition."

"Miss Rutland?"

"No!" cried little Jack, with a snap in her eye.

"Buck?"

"Reckon I'd ruther stay whar I am awhile longer, though, by golly, I'm mighty hungry." He spoke the last words very ruefully.

"Ginger?"

"I ain't no traitor-man, mars', ef I air black. Ginger hain't gwine t' talk 'bout gibben nobody up t' save hisself."

"My friends," I said, and I could not re-press a tremor in my voice, though God knows I tried, " I cannot accept your sacrifice. The guerrillas, having secured me, will doubtless quarrel about you, and the captain and those who are with him may find an opportunity to let you get away under cover of the night."

"No! no!" cried all. "We'll stand to-gether."

" How were you to reply?" asked Helen.

" If the terms were accepted, we were to go down; if rejected, we were to wave."

Helen took off her check bonnet, and, ty-ing it to a carbine, stood up on the rocks and waved it to the guerrillas, who were standing below watching for our signal, while our little command gave as lusty a cheer as their ex-hausted condition would admit.

But the real heroism was yet to come. I had seen evidence that the woman wing of my army was not to be appalled at any propo-sition, but it was impossible that I could be prepared for what was to follow. I have sometimes wondered if it was not rather an emanation of genius than heroism, but have invariably concluded that it was the genius of heroism.

The first flush of excitement at the rejection
of the terms being over, Jack began to show
signs of irritation—a condition I attributed to
the gnawing pangs of hunger. She shook her
fist at the guerrillas, vowing that if she could
ever get her papa again he should scour the
country till he had captured every one of
them, and when captured she would herself
take inexpressible pleasure in making targets
of them for pistol-practice. Then she would
call to them for something to eat. They were
too far to hear her, and, of course, her request
would not have been granted if they had.
"Captain! good captain! dear captain!" she
cried, "do let us out of this; that's a dear
boy." Then she turned to Miss Stanforth.
"Helen, what in the world did we come on
such an errand as this fo'? Why didn't we
send the soldiers?"

"Jack," said Helen, "I'm sorry you regret
it. *I* don't; I never regret."

"Yo're showen' the white feather," said
Buck.

Jack's eyes glistened with anger.

"The white feather! What do yo' mean, yo'
little pest? White feather! I'm not afraid of
all the guerrillas in Christendom. They won't

hurt *me*. I'm going down there to ask 'em fo' something to eat. I'll get yo' all off. White feather! I'll show *you!*"

She sprang upon the rampart, but I caught her and dragged her back.

" Let me go !" she screamed.

" Didn' I tole yo' Missy Jack hab de biggest temper in de Souf ?" cried Ginger, proudly.

" Let her go," said Helen, " and I'll go with her. If those of the guerrillas who are disposed to protect us can do so they will succeed as well without you as with you. Indeed, your presence will only tend to irritate them. Come, Jack, we'll try it."

I stood aghast at such a plan. I forbade it. The girls were determined. I begged, ordered, stormed at them, declaring that for every step they took towards that den of hell-hounds I would take two. At last Helen laid her hand on my sleeve and looked me calmly in the eye.

"Major Branderstane, I want you to let me have my way in this matter. You owe it to me. When you were wounded I took you in and succored you. Since we have been in this place I have obeyed your every order. Jack has flashed out unknowingly, unintentionally, a stroke of genius. Jack *is* a genius. She has hit on our only chance. She fascinated the guerrillas once, and she'll do it again. She will split them in halves, and set one-half against the other. But she will need *me*. Give me that revolver."

All this was lost on me. I swore they should not go. I planted myself between them and the rampart. Helen stepped to one side of me, Jack darted to the other. Ginger put his hand on my arm.

"Don't stop Missy Jack, mars'. Missy Jack can do eberyting wid men-folks." He turned my face to the cliff. "Look dat a way, an' yo' won't see hit."

When I broke from the old man Helen and Jack were beyond the rampart.

I have seen lifeboat-men pull out in a tempestuous sea, breasting a howling wind and madly tossing billows. I have seen men march out to battle with almost a certainty of death or mutilation, but I have never looked upon any sight with the mingled terror and admiration that thrilled me as I beheld these two girls, without other weapon than woman's loveliness, descend the rocky slope towards the guerrilla camp. They moved, hand in hand,

as I have seen graceful ships sail side by side.
Helen was the taller and the more commanding, but both walked erect; Helen buoyed by
a native courage, Jaqueline confident in the
possession of a gift, a genius for bending men
to her will.

They had scarcely left us when the guerrillas caught sight of them and stood looking
up in stupid wonder. Ginger, Buck, and I
were staring down upon them, Ginger's eyes
starting out of his head, Buck leaning ex-
citedly over the rampart, I clutching my carbine. On went the girls, between the flanking rocks, out upon a gentle swell, through a
slight depression, over stones, weeds, brambles,
till at last they came within fifty yards of the
guerrilla camp. Then came a cheer from the
bandits—I knew not whether of triumph or
welcome—and the girls entered the camp.

What they said, what was said to them, I
could not hear—I could only see. Captain
Ringold raised his hat and stood with it in his
hand. He was evidently speaking, for the
men gathered round, and all seemed to be intent on him and the girls. Then I saw Helen
step a little to the front, and all faces were
turned to her. Occasionally she made a gest-

ure, now turning to our little fortress, now pointing the finger of scorn at the guerrillas, as though to shame them or to influence whatever of manliness there might be in them. She was making them a long speech—at least, it seemed so to me, who could see but not hear. At last there was a cheer. The conference was ended.

Then the little actress, Jaqueline, was evidently using her art. She would whisk up to one of the men, stand before him in a favorite position of hers, bent slightly forward, and shake her finger in his face. All the men stood watching her. Occasionally there came a burst of laughter, a yell of applause, a clapping of hands, and I knew that Jack was carrying her audience.

Then I could see the figures below beginning to busy themselves about preparations for supper. Helen and Jack took hold as they had done once before, the men permitting them to do the work.

Buck, beside me, chuckled.

"What is it, Buck?"

"That consarned Jack's goen' roun' thar with the skillet in one han' and chawen' somep'n she's got in the other. Wish I was thar."

When supper was served each man vied with the others to provide for their guests. Jack was seated on the ground, her back resting against a tree, a plate in her lap, a tin cup at her side, evidently making a hearty supper, keeping the men running back and forth from the fire, filling her plate or her cup at every trip.

After supper we could see that the conference was resumed between Helen and the guerrillas. She was evidently arguing with them to effect a purpose. The captain had a good deal to say, but all were taking part in the debate. Then the girls started for our fort. One of the men approached the captain and shook a fist in his face. The captain knocked him down. Another started after the retreating party, but was intercepted. A general fight ensued, some of the men placing themselves between the others and the girls, who were now coming up the hill, quickening their pace at every step. Cocking my carbine, I ran down to join the girls, meeting them midway between the fort and the guerrilla camp. First Jack came dashing past me, wild with terror, her cheeks blanched, her eyes staring. Helen came on more slowly, turning

occasionally with hot cheeks and flashing eye.
Below among the guerrillas was a babel—
swearing, howling, and shooting, the protect-
ing party being the stronger and keeping the
others at bay. I put my arm behind Helen,
and hurried her up the steep slope. When we
got to the fort Jack was already there, crouch-
ing behind the rampart, her head appearing
above it, her eyes as big as saucers.

"Goody gracious, what a fool I was to go
down there! Wouldn't do it again fo' anything."

Helen gave me a hurried account of the
visit. On entering the camp the captain had
complimented them upon their bravery, both
in the fights that had occurred and in coming
out unarmed, assuring them—looking ominously at some of the more cutthroat of his
men—that if any man offered them the slightest indignity he would shoot him on the spot.
Helen had replied that whatever they were,
she believed they were brave, and above in-
juring a woman. Then she held up to them
the magnitude of their crimes, and bade them
go and enlist in the Confederate army. She
succeeded in getting an offer of a free con-
duct to all save me; this they persistently re-

fused. After much urging the captain agreed
that we should be let alone till the next morning—a promise on which I placed no reliance.
Helen begged to be permitted to carry me
provisions. This was also refused.

" I did all I could," she said, ruefully, "but
I couldn't move even the captain. They
wouldn't give me a morsel for you."

" Oh, Helen," said Jack, " I'm tired of hearing yo' whine," and taking off her sunbonnet,
out rolled a liberal supply of corn-pone and
salt pork.

" You little thief!" cried Helen, and threw
her arms around her cousin.

A second time my life had been saved, at
least temporarily, by Jaqueline.

XVI

A BUGLE-CALL

THE night passed without an attack. I prepared a fire as before, but it was not needed. Day dawned, and we could see that the guerrillas had made themselves more comfortable, having constructed a rude hut of boughs for shelter, showing conclusively that they intended to wait patiently for the starving process to do its work. During the day the remnant of the provisions Jack had purloined was consumed, and the command was supperless. Again we entered upon a long, weary night. All except myself were so worn that they evinced little care for watching. They were getting benumbed, a condition which comes at last over one hunted for his life. As for me, my position was harrowing. My devoted friends who had made the attempt to rescue me were starving, and, to crown all, Helen Stanforth, who had instigated the

11

attempt, planned it, and led the others into
it, was deceived as to my true character. I
brooded over the situation till I was well-nigh
insane. Then I made a resolve—a resolve
that might free the others, but would end in
my death. I would go down to the guerrillas
and give myself up. It was possible that my
case having been disposed of, Captain Ringold and his adherents would be able to protect the girls, and, Buck and Ginger being of
no moment to the band, all might go in peace.

But there was an obstacle in the way that I
knew would not be easily overcome—the opposition of all my friends. It was hard for me
to go down to my death. How could I bring
myself to do so with all these beloved ones
endeavoring to prevent me! There was one
way by which I might render them less averse
to the plan. By proclaiming the military mission which had taken me to Alabama I might
render myself an object of hatred and contempt. Despite the pain this confession would
cost me, I resolved to make it.

At the moment I took my resolution I looked
up at Helen, who was always my first object of thought before any important move.
She was leaning over the battlement looking

down upon the guerrillas. In her face was a strength, an honesty such as I had never seen before on that of any woman. My resolve dwindled before that heroic countenance. I could not turn her sublime faith in me to detestation.

However, my purpose to end the struggle by my own surrender was unchanged. Rising, I called out in a tone which at once attracted attention and denoted that I had something of importance to say,

" Dear friends!"

All looked at me inquiringly.

" I am going down there to give myself up; then you can go free."

Helen's gaze bespoke not only her astonishment but dismay.

" What yo' going to do that fo'?" asked Jack, quickly.

" Because I owe it to you all to do so."

" I'm goen' with yo'," said Buck.

" You will do no such thing; you must stand by your sister and cousin."

" What d' y' want to leave us in the lurch fo'?" said Jack, impatiently.

This imputed motive brought a fresh addition to my distress. Even with a perfect understanding between me and the others my burden was hard enough to bear; Jack's taunt well-nigh turned the scale. Bending to the cliff, I buried my face in my hands. A soft hand was laid on mine. Helen was endeavoring to uncover my face. I turned and met her gaze—strong, tender, sympathetic.

"Your life is not yours to surrender. You must wait till it is forced from you."

"I would be unworthy of your sublime devotion should I accept any further sacrifice, especially since it can be of no avail."

"By giving up now you would turn all our efforts to nothing. We shall have made a failure that will remain an eternal burden."

"It will be light compared with my self-condemnation when I see you die with me."

By this time Jack had seized my other hand with both of hers.

"Yo' can't go; yo' mustn't think of it. What would we do without yo'?"

"Cease trying to make a coward of me," I cried, "or, by God, I shall go mad."

I sprang towards the rampart.

"Stop!" cried Helen, imperatively. "I own your life to dispose of as I will—I and Jack. Had it not been for me, you would have bled

to death when you received your wound. Had
it not been for Jack, you would have already
been murdered by the guerrillas."

"Yes, and I am not so base as to pull my
benefactors down with me. Stand aside."

"Hark!"

Jack spoke the word in her quick way, pois-
ing her head on one side to listen. She had
heard a low whistle. In another moment it
was repeated, seeming to come from below,
where we had built our bonfire. A figure
was advancing through the gloom, holding
aloft a white handkerchief. I jumped from
the rampart and ran down to meet this "flag,"
which I soon saw was borne by Captain Ringold.

"What do you want?"

"Don't let your women come into our camp
again. Jaycox is back, and he and Halliday
have got the upper hand. I'm powerless."

"Will your men let the women go if I give
myself up?"

"No; stay with them to the last."

"One word more."

"There's no time. I have stolen away, and
if I am missed and it's known where I have
been, I'll be a dead man."

He was gone before the last word was spoken. I returned to the fortress.

"What is it?" cried Jack, expectantly.

"He has lost the power to protect you; he advises me to stay with you to the last."

"Will you?"

"Yes," I replied, with a sigh.

"Thank God!" exclaimed Helen.

Another night of horror; a rising sun, flooding the face of the rocks and our wan faces with a ruddy glow. A more wretched lot of beings could not be found among castaways at sea. We had not slept during the night, for whatever of rest had come to any of us had been rather stupor than sleep. Our cheeks were sunken; our eyes, deep in their sockets, were turned towards the red orb of day, which to our fevered imaginations seemed to be advancing to strike the final blow.

A great change had come over us during the night. Jack alternated between bursts of passion and a devil-may-care spirit, sprinkled with humorous sallies between tears and smiles, which served to lighten momentarily the gloom for the others, but only rendered me more wretched. Buck craved food more than all the rest, and after a few vain efforts to appear unconcerned, took on a ghastly look that cut me to the heart. Ginger spent a great deal of his time in prayer. Helen seemed calm, yet I noticed a strange look in her eye. Up to this terrible morning she had been the mainstay of the party. Under the strain that smouldering fire which burned within her flared ominously. Turning to me, she asked, harshly:

"Are you a Confederate, or are you a— Yankee?"

"What matters it now?"

"I came to save you, understanding you to be a Confederate."

"Would you abandon me now if you knew me to be a Union man?"

She turned away, and I saw that she was weeping. I put my arm about her and drew her head down on my breast. There she wept long and silently. Whether she was unconscious of what she did, or whether her sufferings made her careless, I did not know, but as I felt her heart beating against mine I was conscious of the birth of a new love.

As the sun rose higher it beat down upon us with all the enervating heat of an unseason-

able day. The water dripping back of us alone
sustained and refreshed us. One by one we
would go to the cleft, and, standing under the
cooling drops, receive them in our mouths.
We envied the birds the food they bore to
their nests, and the freedom of those soaring
far above in the limitless ocean of air. Why
could we not be given wings to fly from our
rocky prison? The wrecked are prone to
dwell on hallucinations; so to us came sounds
denoting the approach of rescuers. One would
hear the tramp of armed men; another would
see the white covers of a wagon-train. All
day we were tortured by these fancies, till at
last I ceased to pay any attention to them.

"I hear horse's hoofs," said Buck.

"Oh no, you don't, Buck," I said, laying my
hand on his head.

"I tell yo' I do."

"Listen," said Helen.

We all listened, but so far as I was concerned
there was no unusual sound.

"I hear them, too," said Jack.

It was singular that these two should
agree. I looked anxiously at Helen. My
hearing was not especially acute; if Helen
had heard, I might have thought there was

something to hear. She listened a long while, but no sound came to her.

"It's gone," said Buck.

"So it is," said Jack. "I heard it; I know I did."

I turned away. It was plain to me that they had been tortured by another hallucination. Neither Buck nor Jack heard anything more, and the incident was soon forgotten, at least by Helen and by me, who had heard nothing. We all relapsed into that dreadful waiting—waiting for the time when the fear of death would be overcome by the pangs of starvation. Helen suddenly looked at me, that dangerous light which I had seen before in her eyes.

"Your enemy?" she asked.

"What enemy?"

"The one you came to Alabama to kill."

"I shall never kill him now."

"Do you mean that you abandon your revenge?" She spoke contemptuously.

"With death staring me, staring you and the others in the face—you who have wrecked yourselves in a vain attempt to save me—my private griefs sink to nothingness."

"You *must* be revenged." She spoke as if it

were she and not I who was to be the avenger.

"I remember; you were to help me."

"I *will* help you."

"There is no need; we are doomed."

"We shall live; and you will meet him."

"And then?"

"You will kill him."

"My poor girl, think no more of that. Let
us fix our minds on gentler things; let us hope
for some escape from this dreadful fate."

She sat down on the bare rock, I beside her.
We both looked out upon the setting sun, tint-
ing the mountains with ominous blood-stains,
like those I had seen on the evening I reached
the guerrilla band. Jack was sitting holding
her knees, rocking back and forth; Buck was
lying on his back with his eyes shut; Ginger
had finished a prayer and was rising from his
knees. Suddenly the whole command started
up as if touched by a current of vitality. There
rang out on the still mountain air the clear
tones of a bugle.

There was no hallucination about this sound.
Each note cut the air with scimitar-like sharp-
ness. To our ears, whetted as they were for
some tidings of relief, it was like trumpet

tones from heaven. It echoed and re-echoed through the mountains, each echo fainter than the last, dying softly in the far distance.

Shading my eyes with my hand, peering down towards the road, I saw through a small opening in the trees files of cavalry passing by fours. They were too far for me to distinguish whether they wore the blue or the gray; but it made no difference; either side would, be welcome. Seizing a carbine, I pointed it at the sky and fired.

The bugle and my shot produced a magical effect on the guerrillas. Without waiting to gather anything but their arms, every man of them darted away into the woods. They knew well what would be their fate could we open communication with the cavalry.

"Not a moment is to be lost," I cried to my command; "that bugle-call was an order to halt. We must catch the soldiers before they start again."

Gathering the guns and putting half a dozen cartridges that remained in my pocket, we all left the fort that had served us so well and started down the declivity. Without the inspiration of those bugle notes we could scarcely have crawled away. Now we not only walked, but walked rapidly. Once past the flanking rocks, we turned to the left, skirted the base of the hill, and made straight for the road. I led, and so great was my anxiety to get the others forward that I was constantly getting ahead of them. I saw that Buck was lagging, and I was starting back to help him when Helen stooped, took him up in her arms, and threw him over her shoulder. He kicked so vigorously at this indignity that Helen put him down, and, his fury lending him strength, he at once took the lead beside me. We hurried on, now and again looking back to make sure that we were not followed, climbing over rocks, through ravines, around projecting points, I directing the course towards the spot where I had seen the passing troopers. We had traversed half the distance when there came another bugle-call. It was the order "Forward!"

I could not repress an exclamation of chagrin. I knew the guerrillas heard all we heard, and this last bugle order would probably arrest their flight and bring them back after us.

"Come!" I cried, "we are still in peril."

I dashed on for a short distance, then turned and cast a glance behind me. Helen was marching firmly; Jack was staggering. As I looked she pitched forward and fell. Before I could reach her Ginger had picked her up, and, gathering her limp body in his arms, her head resting on his shoulder, carried her on. The burden, so precious to the faithful old slave, seemed to give him fresh courage, and he pushed on, though with tottering steps.

"I'll relieve you presently, Ginger," I said, "Hold out as long as you can."

We came to a depression, in the centre of which ran a mountain stream; the descent and the ascent on the opposite side were both rocky, and covered with a thick growth of low timber, and difficult to pass. I glanced hastily to the right and to the left, but, seeing no better passage, plunged down the declivity. Buck was now sticking to me like a leech, Helen was just behind, while a hundred yards back Ginger staggered along with Jack. I waited a moment for him to come up, and then led the way into the ravine, intending to take his burden from him when we had passed the stream. Once at the creek, we waded across. In the middle Ginger stumbled and dumped his burden into the water.

The effect on Jack was marvellous. The

cold water brought a reaction which, if not pleasing, was at least beneficial. She flew into a towering passion at Ginger for dropping her, and when I attempted to take her up gave me a box on the ear that made it tingle. Dripping, she dashed up the rise in the ground, storming as she went, and gained the summit before the rest.

Pushing through a level wooded space, we soon came to the road. A bugle ahead sounded the order to trot. Scarcely had its echoes died away when, from the direction of the outlaws' deserted camp came a shrill whistle.

"The guerrillas!" I cried. "It is now a race between life and death."

XVII

FLIGHT

I was at a loss to know what had brought a body of cavalry up into the Cumberland mountains. I learned afterwards that they had come from Shelbyville and were on their way to attack Bridgeport, where the Memphis and Charleston railroad crossed the Tennessee, with a view to burning the bridge. At Tracy City they had heard of a Confederate force moving on their flank to cut them off, and retraced their steps. Buck and Jacqueline had really heard them going southward early in the afternoon. The bugle-calls we all heard so distinctly were sounded on their way back.

"Where did you leave your horses?" I asked, quickly, of Helen as we hurried on.

"In a clump of trees near the road. There it is now." She pointed to a thicket.

Great was my anxiety as I ran to the place designated, to know if the horses were still there. I was doomed to disappointment; they were gone. There was no time for repining over the loss. I must think out the problem of our immediate action, and that instantly. Two courses were open to us. We might follow the cavalry northward, or we could strike out towards the south. Each plan had its advantages. If we followed the cavalry we might succeed in coming up with them, in which event we should be safe; but as they were mounted and we were not, there was little hope of our overtaking them. Besides, the guerrillas would expect us to follow that course. If we pushed south we must abandon all hope of falling in with the troopers, but would doubtless mislead the guerrillas and gain considerable time. We would also be moving towards the homes of the others of the party. I struck out southward.

"What are yo' going that way fo'?" cried Jack.

"It's the way to go."

"Well, go ahead; *I'm* going after the soldiers."

She turned and started northward. I seized her, and, taking her in my arms, carried her along with the rest, she raining a shower of blows from her little fist upon my head. We pressed on without a word, till Jack, either tired of the situation, or becoming sensible of the absurdity of her action, promised that if I would put her down she would go with us peaceably. I set her on the ground in a very disgruntled condition.

"I wish Captain Ringold were here," she muttered, angrily; "he'd make you pay fo' that."

The road was so winding that I did not fear any one behind could see us from a distance, while, should we leave it, our progress would be very slow. I chose to take the risk of being seen, and put as great a distance as possible between us and the outlaws, while they supposed they were on our track in the direction of the cavalry; for I felt sure they would expect us to take that course. We had not gone far before we met a lean countryman on horseback. In a few words I told him of our situation, and begged him if he met the guerrillas to mislead them. When he learned of our starving condition he pulled a small black bottle containing whiskey out of his saddle-bag. I forced every member of the party to drink, and, tossing the empty bottle at the country-

12

man, hurried on. I knew that the stimulant
would avail us but a little while, then would
only make matters worse. Helen walked on,
showing no effect whatever from the potation,
Jack danced along as if she were at a picnic
party, while Buck suddenly became brave as
a lion.

"Don't yo' think, Mr. Brandystone," he
said, with difficulty getting breath enough to
articulate while walking so fast, " we'd better
stop 'n' fight 'em ?"

"I think you'd better stop talking and save
your breath for walking."

" Reckon we better stop," said Ginger, " 'n'
thank de Lawd fo' letten us out o' dat trap, 'n'
pray fo' dem g'rillas 't git los' in de wilderness."

"We can do that while we're walking," said
Helen, "and not lose any time."

"'Spec' de pra'rs on de knees is mo' effica-
cerous," replied Ginger, " but mebbe we don'
need 'em like we did a spell ago."

Still there was no sound in our rear. Helen
asked if I did not think that keeping the road
was pretty risky. I told her that I would
soon give the word to take to the woods.
Coming to a point where there was a turn,

leaving a straight piece of road back of us, I told the rest to go on while I waited and watched. I stood casting glances back till my army reached another turn in advance, then, pressing forward, caught up with them. In this way I kept them in the road and maintained a rear watch at the same time for nearly half an hour. Then the strength of the party, which had thus far been supplied by excitement, suddenly began to droop, and I, feeling that I had used all the energy there was in them, led the way off the road into the heart of the forest. We had scarcely got into the woods when we heard a clattering of hoofs on the road. Whether they were made by the guerrillas' horses or not I did not know, but I felt very sure they were. We waited till they were out of hearing; then every one sank down on the ground.

"Now, Ginger," I said, "it is a good time to give thanks."

Getting on his knees, Ginger poured out the thanks of the party in words that came as smoothly and plentifully as the waters of a running stream. I, being of that persuasion which has for its motto, "Trust in God, but keep your powder dry," and seeing that Ginger was disposed to prolong his thanksgiving indefinitely, got up and started to find a convenient place to hide. I soon struck a little pocket, formed by the coming together of several declivities, and surrounded by thickets. A little runnel passed through it, and, stooping down, I quenched a thirst that was burning me. Returning to the party, I led them to the retreat I had found for them, then left them to go in search of provisions.

It was now quite dark. I walked half a mile, when I saw the lights of Tracy City. Going to the town and selecting a house standing apart from the rest, I marched boldly up to it and knocked at the door. It was opened by a girl, the only occupant of the place, a wild-eyed creature in dingy calico, unshod, her square-cut locks tucked behind her ears. She appeared to be in a chronic state of fright, and evidently thought me one of those men who were going about taking advantage of the absence of restraint induced by war to help themselves to whatever they wanted. I asked her for some food and a few cooking utensils, and when I paid her for them she was struck dumb with amazement. I returned to camp with provisions, matches, a skillet, and a coffee-pot.

Ginger and Buck had gathered a little wood
for the fire. At the inner extremity of the
pocket we occupied was a low ledge of overhanging rock. It projected but a few feet,
and was about the height of little Buck from
the ground. I hesitated for some time whether it would not be dangerous to light a fire
and thus guide our enemies to where we were,
but at last concluded to place the wood under
the ledge and cover the front with boughs.
Driving three stakes into the ground, I placed
the wood under them and lighted it. Then
filling my coffee-pot with water from the
stream, and putting in my coffee, a very pleasant odor soon greeted our nostrils.

But all were too famished to wait for a
cooked supper. Seizing upon some corn-pone
I had brought, the others devoured it eagerly,
I restraining my appetite long enough to put
some bacon into the skillet. One article of
food after another was devoured as it was got
ready, and our coffee without milk came in at
the end like the last course at a dinner.

As soon as we had finished our supper we
put out the fire, lay boughs where it had been,
and covered them with dry leaves, making a
bed for the two girls and Buck. Ginger was

to bivouac wherever he liked, while I proposed to watch.   Leaving the others to get to bed, I took a carbine and walked towards the road.

There was a light step behind me, and, turning, I saw Helen coming.

"Go back," I said, "and take your rest. You need all you can get."

"I wish to take half your watch."

"You shall do no such thing."

"I am strong; the supper has revived me."

"Helen," I said, quietly, at the same time taking her hand, "I am in command; as a good soldier it is your duty to obey."

I led her back to the camp.   As we passed, hand in hand, over the dead leaves and crackling twigs, my heart was filled, even in our peril, with a supreme happiness, yet a happiness marred by the gulf between us.   I longed to tell her that I loved her—for her bravery, her strength of character, her devotion, for herself—but I could not without confessing myself an enemy to all she held dear.

When we reached the camp we stood face to face in the moonlight.   It seemed as impossible to restrain the words I would utter as it was impossible to utter them.   I dropped her hand and walked away to resume my watch.

From an eminence I turned and looked back. She was still standing in the moonlight. I knew that she was disappointed that I had withheld an expression of my love. What could I do? Turning again, I passed in among the trees.

All through that long night I walked with a soft tread, hearkening to the slightest sound, straining my ears whenever a breeze rustled the branches of the trees, or starting when I heard some fur-coated creature prowling in search of food. Yet during my watch one picture was ever present before me. All night I saw Helen standing in the moonlight, all night I brooded over the barrier that separated us. At dawn I felt that I must get some rest, or I would not be able to lead the party farther. Going to the little camp and awakening Ginger, I led him out to where I had been watching, and told him to keep moving back and forth a short distance from the road, and in case of danger raise the alarm. Then, returning to camp, I threw myself on the ground and fell asleep.

XVIII

RETAKEN

I was awakened by the kick of a heavy boot, and, opening my eyes, looked into the face of Tom Jaycox. The expression of fiendish joy that shone through anxious caution froze the very marrow of my bones. The muzzle of his revolver was within a few inches of my forehead, and his look told me that a word of alarm or a motion for self-defence would be a signal for a bullet to go crashing through my brain.

" Git up," he whispered.

I stood on my feet.

" Move on."

It was the dawn of a beautiful spring morning. The perfume of young verdure, the twitter of birds, an occasional cock-crow in the distance, gave me the thought that it is delightful to live. But they threw over me as well a contrasting gloom, for it seemed certain

that this fair scene was the last of those pictures drawn by the divinely artistic hand of
the Creator that I should ever look upon. My
companions were all wrapt in a heavy slumber,
induced by a long period of unrest. I bade a
mute farewell to each as I passed, breathing
a blessing on little Buck, whose arms were
clasped about his sister, his young face and
figure relaxed; on Jaqueline, her white face
resting in a profusion of tumbled black hair;
on Helen, her features strong even in sleep.
There was a line between the lids of Helen's
eyes; but I thought little of that, for it is not
unusual for people to show this line when
sleeping. I thanked God that my presence
would no longer be a menace to these dear
ones who had suffered so much for me.

Jaycox marched me out of the camp towards the road, across it, and into a wood on the
other side, where his horse was picketed to a
tree. He was constantly looking about and
listening, and I inferred this was for others of
the gang, who had doubtless separated in order
to cover more ground in their search for us.
Finally the brute stood still, and, pointing his
revolver straight at me, fired two shots in rapid
succession, the bullets singing close to my ears.

He did not intend to kill me, though he was indifferent whether he did or not; he wished to serve a double purpose of signalling the band and intimidating me. Two similar shots were fired far to the north, and then my captor started off with me in that direction.

Entering the road we proceeded, Jaycox, some ten yards behind me, amusing himself by firing occasional shots at me, evidently trying to see how near he could come to me without hitting me. One of his bullets grazed my ear, and I felt blood trickling on my collar, good evidence that he had missed his imaginary mark on the wrong side. He was doubtless firing for his double purpose of letting his companions know of his whereabouts and of torturing me. His signals and those of my other enemies were drawing nearer and nearer together. I did not doubt that the guerrillas would prevent any further opportunity for escape by murdering me at once, though they might delay long enough to force me to sign for a ransom which would have no effect in saving me. I lost all care whether Jaycox hit me, or whether I was spared for a more horrible death by the gang. At last I was face to face with the inevitable.

I was trudging on mechanically, my eyes bent on the ground, Jaycox close behind swearing and shooting at me, when suddenly a shot rang out from behind us both. I turned and saw Jaycox tumble from the saddle. Running to where he lay I bent over him, and knew at once that I looked into the face of a dying man. He gave me one malignant look, a shiver passed over him, and his eyes were set in death.

I looked up, and saw Helen standing in the road a short distance back with a carbine in her hands. There was something in the expression of her face, holding as she did the weapon, a light smoke curling from its muzzle, that brought vividly before me my enemy with his smoking pistol on the night of the massacre. A signal shot came from around the trees so near that we knew the rest of the band would soon be upon us. Quick as thought I sprang into the saddle left vacant by Jaycox, and spurred towards Helen, she darting into the wood, I following, and, after penetrating far enough, both hiding behind a rock covered with brush.

A horseman came dashing down the road, pulled up beside Jaycox's body, looked around anxiously as though fearing an ambush, then hurried back whence he came.

With one impulse Helen and I sprang into each other's arms. Oh, the rapture of that embrace! I essayed to speak to her, to utter even a word, an exclamation expressive of what I felt. I could only draw her cheek down against mine and mutely hold it there. Then I showered kisses on her lips, her cheeks, her forehead, her eyes. For the moment I forgot all but the reverence, the gratitude, the burning passion, that thrilled me—a passion such as comes but once, if ever, in a lifetime.

Suddenly there came to Helen a remembrance of our danger.

"Mount! quick! All depends on putting space between you and those who will kill you the moment they get their hands on you again!"

"And leave you? Not I."

"Oh, my God! are you going to act that way again?"

"You have killed Jaycox and released me a second time. Do you suppose they will overlook that?"

She became frantic at my opposition.

"You fool! you ingrate! to throw away your life when I have twice saved it."

"We will go together. Here, put your foot in my hand. Once in the saddle you can ride away, while I can go as fast on foot as you."

"Hark!"

There were sounds of horses' hoofs coming leisurely from the south, and in another moment a mounted man in Confederate uniform emerged from behind the trees, loitering along, the picture of indolence.

"Look!" said Helen, her eyes fixed eagerly on the advancing figure. "It's—"

"Captain Beaumont, as I live!"

Never for a moment doubting that he was followed by his troopers, and infinitely preferring to fall into his hands rather than into the guerrillas', I hailed him. He reined in, stared at us, recognized us, and, after sitting for a moment in mute astonishment, rode towards us.

"What in the name of—"

"Your men — where are they?" gasped Helen.

"I have no men. I sent them back yesterday. We have hunted you fo'—"

"Then dismount, captain," I said, "and be

quick. There are guerrillas up there. They may murder you as well as us."

"My dear man," he said, dismounting leisurely, "yo' are always in a hurry. By-the-bye, where is that fascinating little creature—"

"Oh, captain," cried Helen, "a life — both our lives are at stake!"

"What can I do fo' yo'?" asked the captain, at last impressed with our excited appearance.

By this time the guerrillas had come up to Jaycox's body, and stood alternately looking at it and casting glances into the wood on either side of the road. They raised him, felt of his heart, knew that he was dead, and dropped him.

"It's Jaycox," I whispered to the captain. "He kidnapped me to-day a second time. This brave girl followed and shot him. In a few minutes they will scour the wood. We have but one horse. It will never carry us both swiftly enough for escape."

"I relinquish my horse with pleasure, of co'se. May I assist—"

Helen's foot was in my hand and she in the saddle before he could finish; then I sprang upon the other horse.

"Would you oblige me," the captain called

after us, as we hurried away, "by informing me where I can find that little beauty—"

"Over there—in a pocket between knolls—half a mile—tell them we'll join them later."

I can see him now, with his hand on his heart, bowing profoundly, and, notwithstanding a shudder at remembering the danger we were in, cannot repress a smile at the comical situation of this man who a few days before had ordered me out to be shot, then had offered to lend me money, and now, giving me his horse to save my life, was about to start off hunting for Jacqueline in the Cumberland mountains.

Helen and I, riding side by side, dashed through brush, between trees, over rocks, runnels, rotting trunks of trees, our only thought to put space between us and our enemies. She was riding on a man's saddle, sidewise, luckily supported by a high pommel and holster, keeping her balance as if bred to the "ring."
I reached out my hand; she gave me hers to press, and a lover's look, intensified by our danger, shot between us. It was only for an instant, for so rough was the ground, so numerous the obstructions, that we were obliged

to keep our eyes constantly fixed ahead. There had been exciting moments since my first abduction, but nothing like the wild exhilaration that thrilled me now. I forgot the barrier that was still between us, thinking only that if this one ride were successful years of happiness might be in store for us.

Wondering if we were followed, I drew rein and listened. We could distinctly hear the brush breaking in our rear. Again we pushed forward.

It occurred to me that we were going directly from our camp, and that the greater chance for safety, both immediate and ultimate, would be in hiding, with a view to inducing the guerrillas to pass us, thus affording an opportunity to return and join forces with our friends. Approaching a clump of wood skirted by open ground, a plan flashed through my brain to utilize both in order to elude our pursuers.

" Your bonnet!" I cried to Helen.

She tossed it to me.

" Now ride straight for that thicket."

Spurring my horse to the utmost, I made a circuit, dropping the bonnet, and, a trifle farther on, my hat. Helen entered the wood, and I, wheeling, dashed in on the farther side, and rejoined her. Jerking off my coat, I wrapped it about my horse's ears and eyes to prevent his neighing to those approaching, and Helen, divining my intention, did the same to her own mount with her jacket. Then we stood waiting, not a sound escaping from either us or our horses, even their panting deadened by the covering. It was either life or death, with the chances in favor of death. We stood, hand in hand, looking straight into each other's eyes. In that moment of supreme suspense it was as if but one being waited for the result.

An exclamation: they have seen the bonnet! A shout: they have come upon the hat! They clatter on. Wait. A man in the rear is coming. He too passes, his horse's hoof-beats dying in the distance.

Leaving the thicket, we made straight for the camp, and in a few minutes dashed in upon our companions.

XIX

BUCK'S INDISCRETION

Captain Beaumont had arrived but a few minutes before us, and when we appeared was attempting to reassure Jack, who had completely collapsed at finding that both Helen and I had disappeared. He went to Helen and politely offered to assist her to alight.

"We must move out of this at once," I said. "All depends upon our getting down the mountain and into some town, where these villains will not dare follow us. All stay here while I reconnoitre."

I had not dismounted, and spurred my horse a few hundred yards westward, where I paused on the verge of the plateau. The sun was rising at my back, and was pouring a flood of light on the lowlands a thousand feet below. I swept my eye over the rolling fields and woodland dotted with towns, villages, hamlets, and many a fair plantation with its manor-house surrounded by the huts of the field-hands. Far in the distance was a snakelike line in the road, moving forward, it seemed, as a reptile crawls—the cavalry that we had so nearly caught the day before, now on their way back to join the main force. I longed for a speaking-trumpet sonorous enough to reach them, but there was no hope for us now in them, and I brushed away disappointment and made a survey of the ground directly before me. Nothing but steep incline, so thickly wooded that the character of the ground was completely hidden. On either hand was a mountain spur, between which ran a creek. I hesitated between taking one of these spurs and following the bed of the creek. On the spurs we might be seen; by the creek we would be concealed under the trees. I decided in favor of the latter. Returning to camp I informed the party of my decision.

"Will you join us, Captain Beaumont?" I asked.

"I've been hunting fo' yo' all fo' days," replied the captain, looking at Jack. "Now I've found yo' I'm not likely to part with yo'! Together we can whip the guerrillas."

"Not a dozen of them. Besides, we've had enough of that."

"What are you going to do with the horses?" asked Helen.

"Mount the ladies," suggested the captain.

"Thank yo'," observed Jack, "I don't care to ride on a horse with his nose pointing to China and his tail at the stars."

"No one could ride a horse over such a route," said I. "I'll take care of the stock."

I tethered them in the little pocket we were leaving, knowing that they were less likely to betray our whereabouts to our enemies there than if I turned them loose.

"They'll starve," Jack remonstrated.

"I can't help it."

"They shall not!"

"Come, we have no time to lose."

But Jack set about collecting what little grass was to be had and piling it before them. The captain, seeing her determination, was soon on his knees gathering grass and throwing it in her apron.

"I hope the delay will not cost us our lives," I grumbled. "Now, Ginger, I want you to go off to the right just as far as you can, and still keep me in sight. Buck, you go to the left and do the same, but keep close, for it won't do for us to call to each other."

"Jack can make all sorts o' noises—cats, 'n' owls, 'n' birds—so yo' can't tell 'em," Buck volunteered.

"Good! We may have occasion to use her. You girls keep behind about the same distance as our flankers. When we get to the creek Ginger is to work down it on the right bank, Buck on the left, while I keep as near the creek as possible. Captain Beaumont, will you act as rear-guard?"

"With pleasure, sir."

"He'll go to sleep," remarked Jack, "and be left behind."

"Not with you in front," said the captain, looking at her reproachfully.

I gave the order to move. Making as little noise as possible, keeping each other in sight, except occasionally when the trees and underbrush were too thick, we proceeded to the brow of the plateau. Descending, we soon struck the creek, and under cover of the trees proceeded downward in open order, walking rapidly, keeping a sharp lookout ahead and on the flanks. We had not gone far before an owl hooted behind me, and so natural was the cry that, had I not been expecting it, I should never have suspected it to have come from the

throat of Jaqueline. Turning, I saw both girls
pointing upward. On the very edge of the
declivity, and not far from where we had be-
gun our descent, a man was looking down
from the plateau. We were so protected that
he could not see us, for, besides being among
the trees, we were in comparative shadow,
while the man above stood out boldly in the
light. He did not look like a guerrilla, but we
hurried on.

Discovering a great advantage in Jack's
signals, I called in the flankers and the rear-
guard, and arranged with them that Jack was
to travel with me as trumpeter. The hoot of
an owl would mean "hide"; a woodpecker's
rapping, "rally on the centre"; the notes of a
thrush, "take a back track"; a hen's cackling,
"push forward in haste." These signals being perfectly understood, we opened again, and
advanced like a central sun and satellites.

We had made the principal part of the descent, when, coming to a convenient spot, I
ordered a halt for rest, feeling a confidence
that I had not felt since my abduction—a confidence I should not have yielded to, for we
were yet far from safety. The place of our
halt was a delightful angle in the stream we

were following. Jack strolled away in search
of wild flowers, and was soon joined by Captain Beaumont, whose infatuation prevented
him from thinking of aught else, even our
common danger. Buck stretched himself under a short mountain oak, clasped his hands
under his head, threw one leg over the bent
knee of the other, and looked straight up into
the branches. Helen and I were thus left
alone. We sat down on the bank of the creek
in view of the bubbling stream. Taking a
slender stick in her hand, Helen began to
thrash the water. I saw that she was troubled, and I knew the cause. The barrier between us, which in a moment of intense excitement had faded out of sight, now loomed up
again as ominously as ever. We sat without
speaking. Jack and the captain were chatting
briskly, every now and again speaking loud
enough for us to hear some word that told of
the captain's enthralment. The silence between Helen and myself grew painful; I could
say nothing to break the spell. I could but
mutely express what I felt. Reaching out, I
took her hand and drew her to me.

A shot!

Looking upward to the plateau, I saw a

horseman dashing off to the spur north of us, whose ridge led to the level ground we were approaching. It was plain that we had been discovered, that the shot was a signal, and the horseman was going to head us off.

The trouble had all come from Buck. I have no doubt we should have given the guerrillas the slip had it not been for his folly. There are certain idiosyncrasies in boys that are as natural to them as for a duck to swim or a robin to fly. Unfortunately, at a critical moment, Buck encountered an incident that called out one of these idiosyncrasies. Gazing into the branches of the tree under which he lay, he espied a bird's-nest. Unluckily he noticed that a rock which admitted of a gradual ascent stood directly under the tree. Climbing the rock, he made his way among the branches, and, leaning far out where the bright sun could shine directly on him, grasped for the treasure. Our enemy, who was at the time watching from the plateau, discovered him.

Calling the party together, I gave the order to push forward; not that there seemed to be any object in doing so, for we must expect to meet our pursuers; but we could not go back, and could not stay where we were. Besides, motion would tend to pull together the faculties of the party, every one of whom was appalled at this relapse into the frightful dangers they had so long endured; though Captain Beaumont showed only irritation at having his tête-à-tête with Jack interrupted.

We had not gone far before we struck a path running parallel with the creek, which led us to a hamlet on a road leading north and south. There were but half a dozen houses in the place, including a small country store and a blacksmith-shop. Before entering the town we consulted as to what we should do.

"Get horses," I proposed, "if there is time."

"Or a horse and wagon," said Helen.

"I reckon we better hide," was Buck's proposition.

"Let's get clothes," suggested Jack, "and dress up like village people."

I looked at Helen. Jack's proposition appeared to strike her with the same force it struck me. Of all things the guerrillas would expect us to do, disguising ourselves and going about the town as if we belonged there would be the last.

"Done!" I said, as we entered the place. "Scatter. Tell the people the guerrillas are after us, and they'll help us. We'll have from ten to fifteen minutes to prepare."

XX

A MASQUERADE

WHAT became of the others I did not attempt to discover. I made straight for the blacksmith-shop and found a smith at his forge.

"My good man," I said, "I'm followed by guerrillas. They'll be in the town in a few minutes. Can't you give me your clothes and let me take your place at the forge?"

He stood with his hand on the handle of the bellows looking at me, while what I said was slowly making its way through his skull.

"Weel noo," he said, at last.

"Scotch—I knew it. I'll be taken before I can make him understand." Then to him: "Do you want to save me from death by guerrillas?"

"Certain, mon."

"Then take off that apron and give it to me at once. Not a moment to lose."

At this juncture the desperate position I was in entered his brain, and he worked quickly enough once he realized what was wanted. I saw a woollen shirt, well begrimed, hanging on a nail, and, seizing it, put it on. Then I took the smith's apron, rolled up my sleeves, smeared my arms with cinders, and looked into a bit of broken mirror resting against the wooden wall to observe the effect. I was disappointed to see that my face belied my calling.

"Your razor!" I exclaimed to the blacksmith.

He went through a door leading from the shop to his dwelling and returned with a razor, soap, and hot water. In five minutes I had shorn my beard, leaving a dark stubble, then, seizing a handful of coke, rubbed out every refined lineament. Taking another look at myself I was pleased to see that my own mother would not know me. Seizing the handle of the bellows, I began to blow vigorously.

"Weel, weel," laughed the blacksmith, "ye mak' a better-lo'ken smith than geentlemon."

"Play your own part well," I replied, "and I have something nice for you at the end of the performance."

It was fully fifteen minutes after we reached the hamlet before there were any signs of the guerrillas, and then three or four rode into the town and asked for our party. Had they seen us? Which way had we gone? and other questions, which the few people they met responded to with a grunt or a shake of the head. I put my head out to see, and, recognizing one of them, drew back and began to blow my bellows as if my life depended on it. And it did. Presently one of the outlaws rode up to the shop.

"Hello, thar!" he shouted.

"Wall," I replied, still blowing and keeping my face turned from him.

"Seen a man, two women, a boy, 'n' a nigger go through the town?"

"Hain't seen no one."

"Sho'?"

"Sho' nuff."

He rode off, but I knew the storm had not yet blown over. I went on working the bellows, and it was well I did so, for presently more of the band rode into town, and one of the horses having lost a shoe, its rider dismounted in front of the shop and told me to put it on.

This was something I had not counted on. I knew no more about horseshoeing than about knitting, but I put a bold face on the matter and went to work.

"What the —— you doen'?" yelled the man. "Air y' goen' ter put that shoe on with nary trimmen'?"

"Don't y' s'pose I know my business?" I cried, bristling. "I was only fitten' it."

With that I seized a knife and began to cut. But I was too excited to pare the hoof even if I had been an expert, and in another moment the man yelled again, "Ef yo' cut that critter's hoof off I'll brain yo'."

"Here, Sandy," I cried to the blacksmith within, "come shoe this man's critter; he thinks he knows more 'n I do about shoe'n'."

The blacksmith finished the job while I, pretending to be greatly irritated, was glad to escape into his dwelling-house. Going to a front window and dropping a curtain so that I could look into the road without being seen, I took a view of the situation. The guerrillas were scattered about the town, some riding around the houses hunting for us, others sitting on their horses, questioning the inhabitants as to our whereabouts. Captain Ringold was in command. A negro boy was playing "hop-scotch" on the sidewalk. The captain called to him:

"Yo' boy thar! Didn't yo' see anybody go this way a while ago?"

"Two women 'n' a boy 'bout 's big 's me?"

"Yes."

"'N' a white man 'n' a colored man?"

"Yes; which way did they go?"

"Dey's gwine right 'long dar;" and he pointed to a path leading across the road westward.

"Here, you," cried the captain to two men who were watering their horses at a wooden trough in front of the shop, "strike out on that path."

The men darted away, leaving the captain alone in the road. A little old woman came out of a house opposite and began to guy him in a cracked voice, poking fun at him for not being able to catch a party of women. She talked so familiarly with him that I began to suspect she knew him. I trembled for fear she would betray us.

"You uns ain't wo'th a persimmon," she said; "with them critters' legs under yer, y' orter ketch wimmen folks easy."

"We'll catch 'em easy enough; they've gone along thar," pointing to the path his men were just dashing into.

"Th' didn't go that a-way."

"They didn't? Which way did they go?"

"D' y' s'pose I give fac's fo' nothen'?"

A cold chill ran down my back; she was going to tell for pay.

"What do yo' want?"

"Gimme 'nuff fo' a caliker dress 'n' I'll put yer on th' right track."

"Sho'?"

"Sart'in."

"This 'll git it as easy." He drew a revolver and put it to her face. She drew back. But this man, who was above his calling, never could persist in ill-treating a woman, and, lowering his weapon, he put his hand in his pocket and pulled out a bill.

"That's the stuff ter git fac's with," said the woman. "Now you uns git right 'long thar," and she pointed up the road northward.

"That won't do," said the captain; "we just came from up thar."

There was a pause, at the end of which I heard the woman say, in a low tone:

"Captain!"

The voice was familiar. I saw the man start, then exclaim, "Great God!"

The old woman went over to him, and, taking hold of his bridle-rein, began to whisper to him earnestly. Presently I heard the captain say:

"I can't do it."

There was more whispering, and by the woman's attitude I knew she was pleading. Was she pleading for us? If so, who could this good friend be to take so much interest in us?

"I'd do 't fo' yo' and yo' friend, but not the other one."

She fumbled with the rein, she stroked his horse's neck, she laid her hand on his, all the while talking earnestly and looking up into his eyes, I fancied beseechingly, though I could not see her face, for her back was towards me, while the man's head was drooping lower and lower. Her bonnet fell back on her neck, and I knew the old woman was Jaqueline.

"Can yo' refuse when *I* ask it?" she said, loud enough for me to hear.

The man was silent. The struggle within him was plain in every line of his face. At last he said:

"Fo' yo' sake, little one, I'll do it."

14

She took his rough brown hand in her little white one and bent her head down upon it; then looking up through tears: "I can give yo' only a trifle in reward, captain dear; kiss me."

Bending from his saddle, he reverently touched his lips to her forehead.

Lost in wonder at the strange sight, I was nevertheless congratulating myself that she had secured the man's promise to draw off his force, when the whole advantage was spoiled through the insane jealousy of Captain Beaumont. It seems that the captain had disdained to hide with the rest; indeed, he had no occasion to hide. The guerrillas did not know that he was with our party, and he was in no more danger from them than any other man would be. He had, however, yielded to Jack's persuasion to go into a house and keep out of sight. When the guerrillas rode into town he was sitting by a window sipping a glass of Tennessee whiskey, and at the moment Ringold imprinted the kiss on Jack's forehead, as ill-luck would have it, he happened to look out of the window. In another moment he was in the road, discharging his revolver at the guerrilla, who, drawing his own weapon, returned the fire. A fusillade followed, Ringold receiving a wound that put him *hors de combat*. Swaying in his saddle, he fell fainting to the ground.

Jacqueline turned upon Beaumont like a fury. I have seen little Jack in many a towering passion, but never anything like this. Her face was livid, her eyes flaming. She tried to speak, but her ire choked her. At last, one word expressive of her pent-up feelings came out like a pistol-shot:

"Pig!"

Having thus relieved herself to Captain Beaumont, she turned to the prostrate Ringold, knelt beside him, crooning over him as if he had been dearer to her than all the world beside.

At this moment a guerrilla, who had doubtless been attracted by the firing, dashed down the road. Beaumont caught sight of him just as Jack had hurled her opprobrious epithet. With an expression indicating that he would prefer death to another such word from the girl who had enthralled him, he started to meet the invader. Shots were exchanged, and the guerrilla fell from the saddle. He was followed by another who shared the same fate, while a

third, perhaps fancying that he had struck a
troop of Confederate soldiers, turned and fled.
All this happened so quickly that no one but
Beaumont and the three bandits had an opportunity to take a hand in the fight. When
there were no more guerrillas for the captain
to kill, he went shyly back to Jack, who had wit-
nessed his feat, looking like a school-boy who
had done penance for a fault and wanted for-
giveness. But Jack turned her back on him.

When the firing began, with one bound, disguised and begrimed as I was, I cleared my
window. When Ringold fell I was joined by
the other members of our party from the
houses. Buck had blackened himself for a
negro, and it was he who had answered Ringold's questions. Helen and Ginger had hidden without disguise. The people of the town,
one man and eight women, besides children,
rushed into the road. I knew well that the
absence of the guerrillas was but temporary—
that they would soon come down on us in a
body.

"We have no time to lose," I cried. "We
must get away at once."

"Where?"

"Anywhere."

Turning to the townspeople, I asked if they could furnish a conveyance.

"I've a horse and wagon in my shed," said the smith.

"Out with it, quick!"

Every one of us took a hand in harnessing the team, and in three minutes, by the clock, we had finished. Then we all tumbled in except Jack, who declared she would never leave her friend Captain Ringold. There was no time to bandy words, so I took her up and tossed her into the wagon, where she fell in a heap. Rising on her knees, she shook her clinched fist at me, and cried to the wounded guerrilla that she would come back to him as soon as she could get away. Meanwhile the blacksmith was driving us down the road, belaboring his horse with the stump of an old whip.

XXI

A STERN - CHASE

A STRAIGHT road lay before us to Decherd, a few miles distant. The place was of too great importance for the guerrillas to dare enter, and if we could reach it before they could catch us we should be safe.

"How much is your horse worth?" I asked the blacksmith.

"A matter o' saxty dullars."

"If you kill him by hard driving I'll give you a hundred, and if you get us to Decherd before the outlaws can catch us I'll make it a hundred more."

"Weel, noo, I don't want to be hard on a mon flyen for his life, and wimmen folk, too; I'll do the best I can, and ask no money."

With that he belabored the poor horse's flanks with the stump of his whip, and sent him galloping onward. There were no springs to the wagon, but we valued our lives too well to draw rein at rut or stone. At one part of the road I feared that if we did not check our pace we would break a wheel, and be left with no means to get on, save our legs. I cautioned the driver to slacken his pace, but hearing, or fancying he heard, the clattering of horses' hoofs behind, without a word from me he applied the lash. Now we bounded into the air, and now we were tossed together like dice in a box.

"Git 'oop, ye critter!" cried the blacksmith, mingling Scotch and Tennessee. "Don't ye know ye're draggen' bonny leddies flyen' for their lives?" and down came the butt of the whip. It was harrowing to see a horse forced to give his life to save ours; but our situation was too critical to warrant any slackening of speed. Jack, who of all our force was usually most frightened at danger ahead, and would fight it most vigorously when face to face with it, for once acted in reverse at seeing the poor brute making leaps that were killing him.

"Stop beating that horse, you brute," she cried, "or I'll beat you," and she sprang forward to seize the whip. I caught her in my arms. She looked up into my face, and burst into tears. Whether it was wholly sympathy

or overstrained nerves I did not know—probably both.   At any rate, I protected her from
the jolting by keeping her in my arms, while
she hid her face so that she could not see the
suffering horse.

"Jack," said Buck, "you're nothing but a
baby."

"Shut up, yo' little nigger!" she cried.

I could not repress a smile at the retort, seeing which, Jack realized the absurdity of it
all, and broke into a laugh, while the tears continued to run down her cheeks.

"Won't yo' let *me* support yo' against the
jolting?" asked Captain Beaumont, ruefully.

"Yo'?   Do yo' suppose I'd let you touch me?
Yo' shot my best friend."

"Do yo' dislike me fo' shooting—a robber?"
asked her admirer, sadly.

"I hate yo'."

Beaumont settled down in a corner of the
wagon in despondency.   After a while Jack
slid down beside him, whereupon he suddenly
lighted up and took as much interest in our
flight as any one of the party.

We were a wild-looking load to the few people who passed us.   Whenever we saw a farm-
wagon coming or going we would shout to its

driver to get out of the way. They must have supposed our horse to be a runaway, for every one quickly turned aside. There are pictures of that ride which I can see to-day, so vividly were they stamped on my memory. An old man with his hands on the handle of his plough gaped through iron-rimmed spectacles; a woman in a check gown and sunbonnet stopped trimming plants in her garden, and stood, with the shears in her hand, to gape at us, as if we were a party of witches who had lit on the earth from the moon, and were making ready to take to the sky again. Negroes, children, country lads faced the road as we passed, and stood wonder-stricken till we were out of sight.

Coming to a rise in the ground where we could look to our rear for perhaps a mile, we were terror-stricken to see a man shoot around a bend in the road at a gallop. In a moment another followed. We could not see if there were any more, for we passed over the summit. Not far below a mile-stone told us that it was one mile to Decherd.

"One mile to their two. Can we not do it, driver?" I asked, quickly.

The only answer was another "Git oop," and renewed hammering on the horse's rump.

The eyes of all were strained to the rear, watching to see just what chance there was, from time to time, between life and death, while I examined the carbines, which we had taken care to bring with us, to discover if they were in good condition. At every rise we could see either one or more men coming like the wind. They had evidently caught sight of us, and were straining every nerve to catch us before we reached Decherd. I told the blacksmith to lay it on hard, well knowing that between us and our pursuers was only the life of his horse. He was raising his whip when the horse stumbled and fell, pitching most of us out of the wagon, fortunately on soft ground. Getting up and running to the prostrate animal I found him stone-dead.

We were still a quarter of a mile from the town, and the guerrillas would be on us in a jiffy. Calling to the others to help, I turned the wagon across the road and directed all to take position behind it. Distributing the guns, we waited the coming of the advance of our enemies. Three men, pretty near together, catching sight of us, drew rein and waited for their comrades. Others soon came up, and I counted seven men preparing to charge us. I was about to give an order as to the firing when I heard an exclamation from Ginger:

"Bress de Lawd!"

Turning, I saw a troop of cavalry carrying the Stars and Stripes riding leisurely from the town. I fired a shot to attract their attention. Suddenly they seemed to take in the situation; I heard the sharp word of command, and saw them coming at a gallop. Glancing at the guerrillas, I saw them vanishing in the distance.

"Saved!" I cried.

"De bressed Lawd be t'anked!" shouted Ginger.

"Gol darn it," said Buck, "ef I'd 'a' had a shot I'd 'a' plunked one of 'em."

"By Jove," remarked Beaumont, staring at the approaching troopers, "I'm a prisoner!"

There was a puff of smoke among the retreating guerrillas, the crack of a carbine, and Jack fell into Helen's arms.

Never was the pleasure of hard-earned success more cruelly dashed at the moment of triumph. We had fought these fiends off for days; we had escaped from them to a coveted protection, and now, at the last moment, they had struck us severely. Jaqueline lay on

the grass, her head and shoulders resting on
Helen's arm, who stanched the blood which
flowed from a wound in her side.   I bent over
her with a groan.   Captain Beaumont for a
moment seemed fired to chase the man who
had shot her, then joined those about the
wounded girl, muttering imprecations on the
guerrillas, and incoherently begging us to save
his little Jaqueline.

"A surgeon!" I cried to the troopers, who
were sitting on their horses looking on.
"Some one go for a surgeon."

"Ride quick!" said the captain in command,
turning to the man nearest him, "and bring
a doctor and a conveyance from the town.
Then to an officer: "Lieutenant, follow those
men, and don't come back till you have captured every one of them.   Take twenty men
with the best horses.   With fresh mounts you
can run them all down."

A man dashed off towards the town and
twenty more after the retreating guerrillas.
Jack lay with her head on Helen's shoulder,
her eyes closed, her face white as a cloth, we
all about her, dreading every moment that the
life-blood would run out.   Presently she opened
her eyes, looked about her, then fainted away.

"Oh, my God!" cried Beaumont, "she's gone."

"Keep off," cried Helen, "and give her air."

"Jack," cried Buck, terrified at her ghastly appearance, "wake up!"

I, with a soldier's knowledge of the thirst of a wounded person, dashed away in a hunt for water. I found a well in a yard on the outskirts of the town, and drawing the staple to the chain that held a tin cup, brought a plentiful supply. Helen was still supporting her cousin. Buck was striding about nervously, with his hands thrust down into his pockets, while Captain Beaumont was kneeling, his eyes peering into Jack's as though by his gaze he would hold the life that he dreaded was ebbing away. I sprinkled water in her face, and she opened her eyes, looking about her as if unable to understand her surroundings.

"What's the matter?"

Curiously enough, the words were the same as those I had first heard her utter when, wounded, I reclined on a sofa at her home.

"You're hurt, Jack," said Helen.

"Am I going to die?"

"Oh no, dear, I hope not."

"Don't die," said Beaumont, in a broken

voice. "Don't leave me; I couldn't bear it."

She looked up into his face sadly. "I have been a bad girl to you, captain. Forgive me."

"Forgive you? I love even your harsh words."

"Oh, Helen," she said, "I hope I won't die."

"You won't, surely, Jack."

"Because if I do, I can't dance any mo' fo' the colored people. Who'll look out fo' 'em, Helen? Papa's away, and no one else cares fo' 'em as he and I do."

"They'll have you with them for many a year, Jack."

An open wagon appeared in the road and drove up beside us. A doctor with a satchel in his hand got down and approached Jaqueline. Making a hasty examination of the wound, he bandaged it, then told us to lift her into the vehicle. The seats, except the front one, had been removed, and their cushions placed on the bottom. Some of the cavalrymen tossed in their blankets, and I smoothed them over the cushions, making a comparatively comfortable bed. We placed little Jack upon it; Helen got in with her, and the rest of us walking beside, the cavalry acting as escort, we bore her to the town and lodged her in a room in the main hotel of the place.

We found the town agog with news of the first day's battle at Pittsburg Landing, and I knew that my general would hold himself ready to co-operate. I determined to join my command at once. Having been assured that Jack's wound would not prove fatal, I arranged for the transportation of the party as soon as she could be moved, then gathered my little force in her room and announced my intended departure.

"I must now bid farewell," I said, "to my little army, every one of whom has become dearer to me than life."

"Like General George Washington," said Buck, "sayin' farewell to his ossifers. There is a picture of it in my American school history."

"Good-bye, Buck; remember to get a book and pencil and break yourself of the habit of saying bad words."

"I will, by thunder!"

"Good-bye, little girl," I said to Jack, bending down and kissing her on the forehead.

" Where yo' going?"

" I?   Oh, I'm going away."

Helen's eyes were gleaming.   " Where are you going?" she asked, repeating Jack's question, though in a different tone.

I had managed to keep my connection with the Union Army thus far a secret.   Now I knew there was no need to keep it longer.

" To the Federal Army, where I belong."

The mute agony on Helen's face told what my disclosure had cost her.   Extending my arms, I cried one word: "Sweetheart!"

" Renegade!" she hissed.

" Helen—dear love—hear me."

She turned her back upon me and swept out of the room.

" *I* like yo', ef yo' *are* a Yankee," Jack cried after me.

I left the hotel, my brain in a tumult. Coming up the road was a little knot of troopers surrounding the guerrillas whom they had run down and captured.   A few hours ago I would have cried out with delight.   Now they were no more to me than if I saw them in a dream.

XXII

HUNTING BIG GAME

It was the morning of the 11th of April, 1862. I was nearing the spot I occupied at the opening of my story, where the bushwhacker had sought to kill me; though then I was alone, while now I was with an advancing army. Five hundred cavalry, a division of infantry, and several batteries of artillery were hurrying down the road towards the beautiful city of Huntsville, lying, tranquil and unsuspecting, a few miles below. The upper edge of the sun was peering above the horizon, gilding the crest of the foot-hills of the plateau on the east, the tree-tops, and the roofs of the neighboring houses. The flowers, which a fortnight before were opening, were now in full bloom. They looked innocently from the gardens beside the road; they leaned lovingly against the pillars of the verandas; from vines trailing over casements

15

they smiled at the rising sun; while the breath of morning was laden with their perfume.

It was the general's purpose to surprise the city, capture the railroad machine-shops and the rolling-stock concentrated there, then make up trains laden with troops, seize a hundred miles of the Memphis and Charleston Railroad on either hand, thus opening communication with the army at Pittsburg Landing on the west, and paving the way for future operations in East Tennessee on the east. The enemy must not be given time to move troops to protect the city, for even should we defeat them, they would destroy the shops, and run off the rolling-stock. All depended on celerity and secrecy.

The evening before we had bivouacked ten miles north of the city. Our scouts permitted no one to go south of us, enfolding all they met, in order that no news of our approach could reach the place we hoped to surprise. Two hours before dawn the command was aroused — not by the fife or the bugle, but by whispering officers — and the march was resumed with no sound save the tread of men and horses and the rumble of artillery.

Within a few miles of the city detachments of mounted men, armed with telegraph-cutting and track-tearing implements, dashed to the left and to the right, to prevent the enemy from sending for troops or running off the rolling-stock. To another detachment which rode among the advance columns was assigned the duty of seizing the telegraph-office.

Boom!

Hark! a gun! It comes from the eastward, not half a mile distant, where the railroad runs parallel with the pike. Artillery is driving back a locomotive. The iron monster shrieks like some wild beast that has met its death-wound.

Boom!

More whistles all along the track, far down to the south, varying in distinctness from a near, loud cry to a distant, faint moan. This is fine hunting—stalking locomotives with cannon. Did any South African sportsman ever strike such game, or hunt with such guns?

Boom! boom! boom! Far and near the shotted guns speak—far and near the metal monsters cry out in terror.

Boom!

All are bagged, except one more daring than

the rest, which runs the gantlet of artillery, and with a round shot flying through its cab speeds out of range.

Meanwhile sashes in the houses along the road are being raised, shutters flung open, and heads put out to learn the cause of the commotion. As guns boom, whistles shriek, and cavalry clatter along the road, followed by men rapidly marching and artillery horses briskly dragging the guns, many a citizen, who the night before had gone to sleep not dreaming of a foe, looks upon the passing armed throng, listens to the sound of the cannon and the shrieks of the engines, and wonders if pandemonium has come.

I am drawing near the Stanforths'. There is the house, with its broad verandas and its peak roof. A knot of people are at the front gate, but I am yet too far to see who they are. Now I can distinguish the turbaned Lib. There is a boy perched on one of the gate-posts. It is Buck. That girl, tall and slender, is surely Helen. As I draw nearer I can see Ginger, his broad mouth stretched in a grin of pleasure at sight of Yankee troops. A figure is sitting in a wicker chair on the veranda—dark eyes flashing in a pale face. It is Jaqueline.

Riding up to the gate, I am out of my saddle almost before my horse has stopped. Buck gives a cry, and jumps into my arms. Ginger grasps my hand.

"By jingo! Mr. Brandystone," cried Buck, "I'm mighty glad to see you. Since I got back after fightin' g'rillas like—"

"Mars', 't's good fo' de eyes t' see yo'," interrupted Ginger, enthusiastically.

"After fightin' g'rillas like a man—"

"What! Mr. Branderstane, and in the uniform of a Federal officer!"

It was Mr. Stanforth. He looked at me surprised—then put out his hand. But I always suspected the old man to be at heart a Unionist.

Buck kept on. "After fightin' g'rillas like a man, I come back—"

"Upon my word!"

Another of the family was expressing surprise to see a former guest with the Union troops. Mrs. Stanforth looked pained, but she had nursed me when I was suffering, and her motherly feelings got the better of her prejudices. I took her hand, and she did not withdraw it.

"I say, Mr. Brandystone," Buck now fairly

shouted, "after fightin' g'rillas like a man, I come back hyar to be follered roun' by that doggone old Lib!"

It was out at last, and the boy looked relieved. I broke away, and, advancing towards Helen, put out my hand.

She turned away from me with contempt.

Fortunately at that moment I espied little Ethel looking at me wistfully, and, taking her up, hid my face and my anguish in her tresses. Then looking up I saw that Jack was waiting for me, and, going upon the veranda, I took both her hands in mine.

"Yo're the only Yankee in the world I want to see," she said, enthusiastically.

"Golly!" cried Buck behind me. Turning, I saw what had surprised him—the guerrillas riding by as prisoners. They had been conducted to Shelbyville by the company of cavalry which had captured them, and were now a part of the procession of men and horses hurrying by. Captain Ringold looked up at us with a melancholy stare. He caught sight of Jack, and I shall remember to my dying day the sad look in his eyes as they rested for a moment upon hers.

The advancing army moved rapidly on, and

was soon a mingled mass of guns and horses
in the distance. The sun - touched bayonets
and flags flashed for an instant, then were lost
in a turn in the road. The region which had
so suddenly been enlivened relapsed into the
quiet of the country.

Jaqueline begged me to go into the house.
I declined. Mr. Stanforth added his invita-
tion.

"Thank you, Mr. Stanforth, but I must rejoin my regiment at once. This is no time for
me to be absent."

"You shall come in long enough to drink
one glass of wine to show that you are our
friend." I saw that he would be not only
hurt, but, with his strong Southern impulse,
angered if I refused, and I reluctantly consented to spare a few minutes to pledge my
former host.

I entered the house supporting Jack, and was
turning into the library, where I had passed
my time while wounded, when Jack guided
me into the parlor opposite. Helen left us
and went into the library. Lib came in bearing a decanter and glasses. I drank to the
host and the assembled company, promising
that during the occupation by the Union forces

I would use my influence to gain them every favor and protection. I had drained my glass and, setting it down, was about to go out to mount my horse when Helen came out of the library and crossed the hall, hand in hand with an officer in Confederate uniform. His forehead was bound with a handkerchief, he walked with difficulty, and I judged had been severely wounded. Jack sprang forward and seized the other hand.

"Major Branderstane," said Helen, "my brother."

Great God! Before me stood—my enemy!

As at night by a flash of lightning one may see for an instant a landscape distinct in all its details, so I saw again the events of the night of the massacre. There were the flashing shot-guns, the soldiers coming down the hill, a figure with garments streaming in the wind running to me for protection. And now before me stood the man with the smoking pistol. Involuntarily I put my hand to my revolver.

"I am your prisoner, sir," he said, quickly; "you do not need your weapon."

Helen's eyes flashed. "Would you shoot an unarmed man?"

Jack, mute with terror, staggered to the gray clad figure and clung to it, her expressive eyes bent on me, a mingled flame of reproach and wrath.

My hand rested on my holster. I moved not—spoke not—but stood staring at the group that stared at me. This man, whom I had been hunting to kill, whom Helen had stimulated me to pursue, against whom she had even voluntarily pledged herself to aid me in my revenge, had now suddenly appeared as her brother.

"I was wounded," said the officer, "at Fort Donaldson, and was brought here to my father's house. I am unable to endure the fatigue of flight, therefore I am compelled to surrender."

"Captain Stanforth, I have been hunting for you for months."

" Me ?"

" You."

" What for ?"

A hush came over all as if about to listen to a sentence of death.

" To kill you."

There was a brief murmur among those looking on, then they stood breathless, waiting for the next scene in what promised to be a tragedy. Only Helen knew what my words meant. I saw a spasmodic quiver pass over her as I had seen death touch a comrade who had been shot in battle. Then, gathering her forces, she stood still, her face denoting the smothered fires of a volcano.

"May I ask, sir," said the officer, pale but calm, "why you desire my death?"

"The wrong, the brutal wrong you did."

I know not why some demon of barbarism should have come to me at this critical moment when, of all others, I should have shown gentleness and magnanimity. Here was an opportunity to make a graceful acknowledgment of Helen Stanforth's service and sacrifice, perhaps to heal the breach between us. I threw it away. My abandoned purpose was rekindled: I was crazed by Helen's treatment. I drew my revolver and brought it to bear on my unarmed enemy.

"Coward!" cried Helen.

I turned to her scornfully. "Who bade me pursue this man to the bitter end?"

"I."

"Who promised to aid me?"

"I."

" Who now begs for her brother's life at the hands of a *Southern renegade?*"

"I? Never." She sprang between me and her brother—" Fire!"

She stood glaring at me, beautiful in her uncompromising fury. I was bewildered, entangled in the meshes of her beauty, her relentless will power. Then suddenly a cold chill swept over me, as a blighting frost across a land hot with the rays of a tropical sun. I stood aghast at what I had done. I had returned her inestimable service by a miserable attempt to force her to beg for her brother's life. I had lost what hope I had cherished of a reconciliation—of winning her. I threw my weapon into a corner and was striding from the room, when Captain Stanforth, freeing himself from Jack, cried :

"In the name of God, what does all this mean ?"

" It means, Captain Stanforth," I said, turning, "that on a certain night in East Tennessee a party of Unionists on their way north were ambushed by citizens with shot-guns. A body of Confederate cavalry came down to their assistance. You, Captain—"

"It is false. I led my company to the

scene you mention—not to attack, but to protect."

It was now my turn to stand stupefied. Had I been all these months following an error?

"I came on the ground," Captain Stanforth continued, "just in time to witness the most diabolical sight I ever saw in the South. One incident of that terrible night I shall always remember—a murder that I punished with my own hand. I saw a woman flying for protection to a man who stood near her. A cowardly cur beside me fired, and she fell through her protector's arms. I drew my revolver and shot the murderer dead."

"*You* shot the murderer?"

I had no tongue for other words. This man, dear to Helen, dear to Jack, dear to all this household, was not only innocent of the crime I had imputed to him, but was my avenger. I took one step forward and seized his hand.

"Thank God!"

"You have been mistaken?"

"So far mistaken that had it not been for these two women I would have shot you down where you stand."

I strode to the door, rushed down the path

to the gate, mounted my horse, and, without once looking back at the gaping crowd behind me, galloped down the road after the advancing army.

XXIII

THE UNION SAVED

I CAUGHT the troops just as they were entering the city. All that we could have wished for was accomplished. The whole territory was surprised and defenceless, and a hundred miles of railroad fell into our hands. Machine-shops, rolling-stock in abundance, telegraph, and all other paraphernalia for operating the line were among the trophies, and on the morning after the capture the men who had been employed under the direction of the Confederate government went to work for the United States.

And now followed a rest for three months, a longer stay in one place than any I experienced during the war. It would have been the most delightful had it not been for my estrangement from Helen Stanforth. Though I was welcome at her father's house, though the family apparently became attached to me, though Jack and Buck loved me as I loved them, Helen remained obdurate. In vain I sought to soften her by those attentions with which men seek to entrap a woman's heart. She would not even treat me with indifference. I was to her a renegade to the South, an unpardonable offender.

I reported the case of Captain Stanforth to the general, and secured from him a parole, which enabled him to divide his time between his father's house and the Rutland plantation with his *fiancée* Jaqueline, who soon nursed him back to health. Captain Beaumont was brought to Huntsville under guard, and I interested myself in securing for him an early exchange, which, after hearing of Jack's engagement, he was extremely anxious to obtain. He was passed through the lines to Chattanooga, vowing that he would give his life to the Confederacy if he could find a Yankee bullet to assist him. He was too manly and chivalrous to cast the slightest blame on Jack for his disappointment.

One morning I took my friends from Mr. Stanforth's — excepting Helen — into headquarters and introduced them to the general. He was aware of our coming, and had directed that the outlaws should be brought before him at the same time.

"Are these the men?" he asked.

"Yes, general," I replied.

To the officer of the guard, he said, "Take them away. *I don't wish to see any more of them.*"

Jaqueline, who had heard these words once before when they were applied to me, and consequently knew what they meant, turned pale. She begged the general to spare them. He shook his head.

"Impossible. They are the crowning barbarity of war."

"But, general, that one," pointing to Captain Ringold—"he helped us."

"Ah! I had forgotten that." Then turning to Ringold:

"If set at liberty, how long will you require to get out of my lines?"

"I will go at once."

"Go; and if you are seen about here after 'tattoo' this evening you will follow your men."

The reprieved man sprang towards Jaqueline, seized her hand, and kissed it. "From this moment I am a changed man," he said to her, "and your bright eyes and kind heart have done it." In another moment he was gone.

Captain Stanforth was soon exchanged, and before leaving to join his regiment was united to Jaqueline. The wedding took place at the Rutland plantation. The groom did me the honor to request me to act as his best man, Jaqueline doubtless having influenced his choice. I gladly accepted, hoping that, since Helen was to serve as· first bridesmaid, our being thrown together might heal the breach between us. Ten minutes before ·the ceremony Jaqueline was strumming Ginger's banjo, and ten minutes after she had become a bride was standing on the rear gallery tossing presents to a crowd of black people below, whose upturned faces indicated the adoration in which they held their young mistress.

I was disappointed in my hope that the festivities would thaw the obdurate heart of the woman I loved. She remained cold, even when her hand was laid on my arm before and after the ceremony. Later, finding her apart from the others, I approached her.

"Have you not one kind word for me?" I asked.

16

"Not one. I can respect a Northern soldier, not a Southern man who wears the blue."

"Be it as you wish."

Mounting my horse, I rode back to camp with a heavy heart.

The advantages gained by our force at Shiloh, and our own bloodless conquest of Northern Alabama, were not vigorously followed up. The enemy withdrew to Tupelo, Mississippi, where he formed a new army, which, early in the fall, marched, under the Confederate general Bragg, through Chattanooga into Kentucky.

One morning in September orders came for us to break camp and march northward. Bragg was advancing, marching on Cincinnati or Louisville, thus compelling the abandonment of the territory we had acquired in the spring, and requiring us to hasten to the protection of the threatened cities. After making my preparations for the move I left the command, intending to join it on the march, and rode over to the Stanforths' to take my leave. Jackson announced me, and I sat down in the little library I had occupied three months before, while my wound was healing, to await the ap-

pearance of my friends. I was startled by the
voice of Buck coming from above:

"Lib, doggone 't, whar's my swearen' book?
I've lost that 'swearen' book' what Major
Brandystone tole me to git."

A few minutes later he came into the room.
As he caught sight of me his face became
radiant, and, jumping into my arms, he hugged
me like a young bear. The others soon entered.
Mr. Stanforth, who by this time had openly
avowed his affection for the Union, parted from
me with regret, not unmixed with apprehension
lest upon the return of the Confederates he
might suffer for his attentions to our troops.
Mrs. Stanforth bade me adieu with motherly
affection. Little Ethel put her arms about my
neck and wondered. Buck, for the moment,
in his affection for me, forgot that he was a
Confederate sympathizer, and insisted on going with me. Helen stood aloof, and at the
last moment seemed more bitter than ever.
There was a flush upon her cheek and a bright
spark in her eyes.

"Good-bye," I said, putting out my hand to
her.

"Never to an enemy," she replied, turning
away.

There was a murmur of disapprobation at her act, but I did not listen to it. Turning on my heel, I left the room and the house, and in another moment was galloping away.

My regiment was moving on a road leading northward and to the east of the main pike, so I was obliged to ride across country to rejoin. Large armies necessarily move slowly, and although in this instance we had entered upon forced marches I knew that I had plenty of time. I was riding leisurely through a lonely road when I heard the sound of horse's hoofs behind me. I had become so used to being hunted by my old enemies that I instinctively drew rein and my revolver at the same time, and, facing about, awaited the coming of friend or foe. My pursuer turned a bend in the road but a short distance from me and suddenly came in sight.

"Helen Stanforth! What in the world brings you here?"

She drew rein and sat with flushed cheeks, her eyes looking anywhere except on me. Her horse was restive, the two making a picture by no means quiescent.

"I am not satisfied."

"With what?"

"The manner of your leaving the country."

"Do I take with me what does not belong to me?"

"You are going with our enemies."

I was puzzled. She knew that I was a Union officer, and that my duty lay with the departing army. Besides, to remain in the country after its reoccupation by Confederate troops would be as much as my life was worth. I was more than puzzled, I was irritated, smarting as I was under her recent treatment.

"This is not what dissatisfies you," I said.

"I spent my time rescuing a renegade."

"I see no occasion for you to come after me to hurl that taunt anew. We parted half an hour ago, I supposed never to meet again. Now you must needs—"

"Were you not in the Yankee service our parting need not be—"

She paused and bit her lip.

I had often noticed a great show of picket-firing on the part of an enemy just before abandoning his lines. Somehow the thought gave me an inkling of what was passing in Helen's mind. I rode up close beside her, and laying my hand on her horse's neck stroked it for a moment till I had quieted him. Meanwhile my eyes were fixed on Helen's, that were glancing about wildly, as if endeavoring to find some means of retreat. Bending forward, without a word, I put my arms about her and drew her to me. Her head sank slowly, at last resting on the embroidered leaves that denoted my rank.

"Sweetheart, I love you, and I believe you love me."

There was silence, save for the running water of the creek and the chattering of the birds in the trees beside the road. The touching of our lips, her heart beating against mine, stray strands of her hair falling over my wrist, the moisture in her eyes, bring a new warmth to my heart even to-day. At last she suddenly disengaged herself and, as though ashamed of her surrender, turned her horse to move away. I caught her and held her long enough for one more embrace, one long parting kiss; then I let her go. As she galloped down the road I called after her:

"You forgive me for threatening your brother—for trying to compel you to beg for his life?"

"No."

"I'll come when the Union is saved."

"When the Confederacy is acknowledged," and she shot around the bend out of sight.

"I believe," I mused, as I rode on, "there is no inconsistency, no incongruity, that does not enter into the composition of woman."

We met again a year later, shortly before the battle of Chickamauga, and again when Hood was marching against Thomas at Nashville, but it was not till after the surrender at Appomattox that she consented to a union that was to be simultaneous with the reunion of the States.

One important fact has always remained a secret between me and my wife. I have never ventured to confess to her that during the war I performed one act of secret service. In overhauling my papers she one day came upon a document gotten up in red and black ink in the form common in the army.

"What's all this about?" she asked. "'Gallant and meritorious services in the capture of Huntsville, Decatur, and Stephenson Junction.' I thought that when the Yankees surprised Huntsville you were at our house."

"That?" I said, taking the paper and pretending to scrutinize it—"oh, that was for capturing a rebel."

"What rebel?"

I hesitated, then prevaricated. "Don't you remember the scene in which your brother bore an important part?"

"Do you mean to call drawing your pistol on an unarmed man a gallant and meritorious act?"

"Oh, they complimented everybody for everything during the war. But I deserved the encomium, for I captured another rebel more rebellious than your brother"

"Who was that?"

I put my arms about her and kissed her.

"My sweetheart."

THE END

By CAPTAIN CHARLES KING.

CAMPAIGNING WITH CROOK, AND STORIES OF ARMY LIFE. Post 8vo, Cloth, $1 25.

A WAR-TIME WOOING. Illustrated by R. F. ZOGBAUM. Post 8vo, Cloth, $1 00.

BETWEEN THE LINES. A Story of the War. Illustrated by GILBERT GAUL. Post 8vo, Cloth, $1 25.

CADET DAYS. A Story of West Point. Illustrated. Post 8vo, Cloth, Ornamental, $1 25.

Captain King's stories of army life are so brilliant and intense, they have such a ring of true experience, and his characters are so lifelike and vivid that the announcement of a new one is always received with pleasure.—*New Haven Palladium.*

In all of Captain King's stories the author holds to lofty ideals of manhood and womanhood, and inculcates the lessons of honor, generosity, courage, and self-control.—*Literary World,* Boston.

A romance by Captain King is always a pleasure, because he has so complete a mastery of the subjects with which he deals. . . . Captain King has few rivals in his domain.—*Epoch,* N. Y.

All Captain King's stories are full of spirit and with the true ring about them.—*Philadelphia Item.*

In the delineation of war scenes Captain King's style is crisp and vigorous, inspiring in the breast of the reader a thrill of genuine patriotic fervor.—*Boston Commonwealth.*

Captain King is almost without a rival in the field he has chosen. . . . His style is at once vigorous and sentimental in the best sense of that word, so that his novels are pleasing to young men as well as young women.—*Pittsburgh Bulletin.*

It is good to think that there is at least one man who believes that all the spirit of romance and chivalry has not yet died out of the world, and that there are as brave and honest hearts to-day as there were in the days of knights and paladins.—*Philadelphia Record.*

PUBLISHED BY HARPER & BROTHERS, NEW YORK.

☞ *The above works are for sale by all booksellers, or will be sent by the publishers, postage prepaid, to any part of the United States, Canada, or Mexico, on receipt of the price.*

By ELIZABETH B. CUSTER

FOLLOWING THE GUIDON. Illustrated. Post 8vo, Cloth, Ornamental, $1 50.

The story is a thrillingly interesting one, charmingly told. . . . Mrs. Custer gives sketches photographic in their fidelity to fact, and touches them with the brush of the true artist just enough to give them coloring. It is a charming volume, and the reader who begins it will hardly lay it down until it is finished.—*Boston Traveller*.

An admirable book. Mrs. Custer was almost as good a soldier as her gallant husband, and her book breathes the true martial spirit.—*St. Louis Republic*.

BOOTS AND SADDLES; or, Life in Dakota with General Custer. With Portrait of General Custer. 12mo, Cloth, Ornamental, $1 50.

A book of adventure is interesting reading, especially when it is all true, as is the case with "Boots and Saddles." . . . Mrs. Custer does not obtrude the fact that sunshine and solace went with her to tent and fort, but it inheres in her narrative none the less, and as a consequence "these simple annals of our daily life," as she calls them, are never dull nor uninteresting. —*Evangelist*, N. Y.

No better or more satisfactory life of General Custer could have been written. . . . We know of no biographical work anywhere which we count better than this.—*N. Y. Commercial Advertiser*.

TENTING ON THE PLAINS; or, General Custer in Kansas and Texas. Illustrated. Post 8vo, Cloth, $1 50.

Mrs. Custer was a keen observer. . . . The narrative abounds in vivid description, in exciting incident, and gives us a realistic picture of adventurous frontier life. This new edition will be welcomed.—*Boston Advertiser*.

PUBLISHED BY HARPER & BROTHERS, NEW YORK

☞ *The above works are for sale by all booksellers, or will be sent by the publishers, postage prepaid, on receipt of the price.*

By THOMAS HARDY

Hardy has an exquisite vein of humor. His style is so lucid that the outlines of a character in one of his books are unmistakable from first to last. He has a reserve force, so to speak, of imagination, of invention, which keeps the interest undiminished always, though the personages in the drama may be few and their adventures unremarkable. But most of all he has shown the pity and the beauty of human life, most of all he has enlarged the boundaries of sympathy and charity.—*N. Y. Tribune.*

UNIFORM EDITION:

THE WELL-BELOVED.	THE TRUMPET-MAJOR.
JUDE THE OBSCURE. Illustrated.	FAR FROM THE MADDING CROWD.
UNDER THE GREENWOOD-TREE.	THE MAYOR OF CASTERBRIDGE.
WESSEX TALES.	A PAIR OF BLUE EYES.
DESPERATE REMEDIES.	TWO ON A TOWER.
A LAODICEAN.	RETURN OF THE NATIVE.
THE HAND OF ETHELBERTA.	TESS OF THE D'URBERVILLES. Illustrated.
THE WOODLANDERS.	

Crown 8vo, Cloth, $1 50 each.

LIFE'S LITTLE IRONIES. A Set of Tales; with some Colloquial Sketches entitled A Few Crusted Characters. Post 8vo, Cloth, Ornamental, $1 25.

A GROUP OF NOBLE DAMES. Illustrated. 12mo, Cloth, Ornamental, $1 25; Post 8vo, Paper, 75 cents.

THE WOODLANDERS. 16mo, Cloth, 75 cents.

FELLOW-TOWNSMEN. 32mo, Paper, 20 cents.

PUBLISHED BY HARPER & BROTHERS, NEW YORK.

☞ *The above works are for sale by all booksellers, or will be sent by the publishers, postage prepaid, on receipt of the price.*

By GEORGE DU MAURIER

ENGLISH SOCIETY. Sketched by GEORGE DU MAURIER. About 100 Illustrations. With an Introduction by W. D. HOWELLS. Oblong 4to, Cloth, Ornamental, $2 50.

A volume which it will always be a delight to have in the house. In it a searching observer of many phases of humanity, charming in its wit and without the blemish of malice, presents with his pencil as much of his social philosophy as he could give with his pen in a hundred novels.—*N. Y. Sun.*

As to the drawings, what can we say in praise of them that has not been said time and again ? The humor, the satire, so effective notwithstanding the light touch, are all here, as they are in everything that Du Maurier drew.—*Critic, N. Y.*

TRILBY. A Novel. Illustrated by the Author. Post 8vo, Cloth, Ornamental, $1 75 ; Three-quarter Calf, $3 50 ; Three-quarter Crushed Levant, $4 50.

Mr. Du Maurier has written his tale with such originality, unconventionality, and eloquence, such rollicking humor and tender pathos, and delightful play of every lively fancy, all running so briskly in exquisite English, and with such vivid dramatic picturing, that it is only comparable . . . to the freshness and beauty of a spring morning at the end of a dragging winter. . . . A thoroughly unique story.—*N. Y. Sun.*

PETER IBBETSON. With an Introduction by his Cousin, Lady * * * * ("Madge Plunket"). Edited and Illustrated by GEORGE DU MAURIER. Post 8vo, Cloth, Ornamental, $1 50 ; Three-quarter Calf, $3 25 ; Three-quarter Crushed Levant, $4 25.

There are so many beauties, so many singularities, so much that is fresh and original, in Mr. Du Maurier's story that it is difficult to treat it at all adequately from the point of view of criticism. That it is one of the most remarkable books that have appeared for a long time is, however, indisputable.—*N. Y. Tribune.*

PUBLISHED BY HARPER & BROTHERS, NEW YORK.

☞ *The above works are for sale by all booksellers, or will be mailed by the publishers, postage prepaid, on receipt of the price.*

www.ingramcontent.com/pod-product-compliance
Lightning Source LLC
Chambersburg PA
CBHW031423020726
47499CB00005B/1575